P9-DGE-892

More to the Story

ALSO BY HENA KHAN

Amina's Voice

It's Ramadan, Curious George

Golden Domes and Silver Lanterns: A Muslim Book of Colors

Night of the Moon: A Muslim Holiday Story

Under My Hijab

Zayd Saleem, Chasing the Dream

Power Forward

On Point

Bounce Back

More to the Story

Hena Khan

Author of *Amina's Voice*

NEW YORK LONDON TORONTO SYDNEY NEW DELHI

An imprint of Simon & Schuster Children's Publishing Division
1230 Avenue of the Americas, New York, New York 10020

Jacket design by Krista Vossen
Interior design by Hilary Zarycky
The text for this book was set in Goudy Oldstyle.
Manufactured in the United States of America
0819 FFG
First Edition
2 4 6 8 10 9 7 5 3 1
Library of Congress Cataloging-in-Publication Data
Names: Khan, Hena, author.
Title: More to the story / Hena Khan.
Description: First edition. | New York : Salaam Reads, [2019] | Summary: As features editor of her school newspaper, thirteen-year-old Jameela Mirza wants to impress her father by writing a spectacular story about the new student, but a misunderstanding and family illness complicate matters.
Identifiers: LCCN 2019001352 (print) | LCCN 2019002752 (eBook) | ISBN 9781481492096 (hardcover) | ISBN 9781481492119 (eBook)
Subjects: | CYAC: Family life—Georgia—Atlanta—Fiction. | Newspapers—Fiction. | Middle schools—Fiction. | Schools—Fiction. | Pakistani Americans—Fiction. | Muslims—United States—Fiction. | Atlanta (Ga.)—Fiction.
Classification: LCC PZ7.K526495 (eBook) | LCC PZ7.K526495 Mor 2019 (print) | DDC [Fic]—dc23
LC record available at https://lccn.loc.gov/2019001352

To my strong and beautiful mother,
who showed me the magic of books

More to the Story

1

"This is the worst Eid ever!" Aleeza flops onto the sofa and grabs the TV remote.

"You'll wrinkle your outfit," Bisma warns.

"I don't care," Aleeza says, then quickly adjusts her kameez beneath her. "It doesn't feel like Eid. Baba's not here. We were supposed to leave for the party like an hour ago. And now we're stuck at home, because people are coming over."

"Your whining doesn't make it any better," I snap at her. She's right that it's been a pretty disappointing day so far. Baba had to fly out for an interview in Maryland early this morning, before the rest of us went to the mosque for prayers. It's our first Eid without him, and everyone's been on edge. But it's only three o'clock in the afternoon. Maybe things will turn around.

"Come on, guys—it's Eid," Bisma pleads. "Can't you be nice to each other today?"

"*She* should be nice. Jam's always mean to me!" Aleeza shakes her finger at me, and her eyes fill up.

So much for things turning around. There's no way to sugarcoat it: My youngest sister is spoiled rotten. Aleeza's only ten, but that doesn't stop her from bossing around Bisma, who's a year older than her. And it doesn't matter to her that I'm thirteen and in middle school. Aleeza doesn't respect me like she should.

"Jameela!" Mama calls to me from the kitchen. "Can you go down and get the nice napkins? From the garage?"

"Okay." I'd rather face the lizards in the garage than listen to Aleeza whine for a second longer. Ever since Bisma saw a baby gecko scamper along the walls and freaked out like it had escaped from Jurassic Park, I'm the only one of us girls who dares to go in there alone.

The air inside the garage is suffocating, which isn't surprising, since it feels like five hundred degrees outside. This year Eid fell in August, the hottest month of the summer. Today also happens to be the kind of record-breaking scorcher of a day that earns Atlanta the nickname Hotlanta.

The jumbo pack of napkins is on a crowded shelf, next

to a box marked "JAMEELA'S STUFF: PRIVATE!!!" where I've stored my old journals and collection of last year's middle school newspapers. I was the only sixth grader who was an assistant editor and had an article in every issue of the paper, so I saved two copies of each. I resist the urge to carry the box inside so I can reread them, savoring each word like I want to.

Out of the corner of my eye I spot a lizard, frozen in place near the garage door opener. I decide it's going to be the subject of a future article in the *Mirza Memos*, the family newspaper I've been writing since I was nine years old. Maybe I'll research whether geckos have ever harmed humans, or how to get over the fear of creatures that resemble tiny alligators. If that includes hypnosis, I hope my sisters will let me try it out on them.

I make sure my box isn't at risk of getting crushed by the endless stream of things that flow out of our town house into the garage. Then I grab a stack of napkins and head upstairs to the kitchen. Mama is arranging mini samosas on a platter, while Maryam cuts the raspberry bars she made into neat squares.

"Can you put those on the table with this fruit?" Mama's brow furrows as she eyes the simple cotton shalwar kameez I threw on for Eid prayers earlier. "Aren't you going to change into your new clothes?"

This morning I hit my snooze button over and over, which left no time to iron the bright green outfit with sparkly gold thread work I'd left crumpled on my floor after trying it on last week. All I needed was a big star on my head, and I would have looked exactly like a walking Christmas tree decorated with tinsel. But since Mama's cousin in Pakistan had sent me the outfit, and because I knew it must have been expensive, I pretended to like it.

"Please say you will," Maryam adds. My older sister is elegant in her silvery-gray outfit with black embroidery. Her makeup, perfected after hours of watching tutorials on YouTube, is flawless. She's wearing a high bun, with wisps of loosened hairs that frame her cheekbones. As she bats her dark lashes at me, I squint at her, trying to tell if they're fake. She looks older than fifteen, and is glamorous.

"It's too hot for silk. Who's coming over, anyway?" I tuck a curl that escaped my ponytail behind my ear and try not to think about how my rolled-out-of-bed look compares to Maryam's. "Why do we need to impress them with fancy napkins?"

"Uncle Saeed. He's bringing his nephew. I'm just trying to make it special for Eid," Mama says.

I perk up when I hear "Uncle Saeed." He's Baba's

best friend, and our dentist. He's always armed with corny jokes and free toothbrushes.

When the doorbell rings, my mother gives me a gentle shove.

"Go change your clothes, and fix your hair, please," she urges. "There's a big stain on your kameez."

"It's fine," I say as I bound down the stairs for the door. "Uncle Saeed won't care. I'll change before the party."

I throw the door open.

"Eid Mubarak!" Uncle Saeed declares. He's holding a light blue box in his outstretched arms, and beads of sweat have already formed on his forehead. "Something sugary for the sweetest of days." Uncle often speaks as if he's quoting a Hallmark card.

"Eid Mubarak." I take the box and scan the label. Yes! It's from Sugar Kisses Bakery. Mama thinks it's overpriced and refuses to take us there. But when I tried their salted-caramel cupcake at Kayla's birthday party, it was literally one of the best desserts I've ever tasted. "Thank you! Come on in."

"Oof. It's too hot today. Eid Mubarak." Farah Auntie manages a weak smile, but her nose wrinkles slightly when she scans my hair and outfit.

"Are you feeling okay?" she whispers before hugging

me three times, enveloping me in the overpowering scent of her perfume. "Such simple clothes for Eid?"

"I'm great." I brush off Auntie's questions, since she's always one to gently point out how I dress too plainly for parties. Or weddings. Or Eid. If I were wearing my tinsel-tree getup, I'm sure I'd hear "Oh mashallah, *today* you look nice," no matter how uncomfortable or sweaty I felt. I've learned to let her and the other aunties comment about me, and then gush over Maryam. She puts enough effort into dressing up for both of us.

Uncle clears his throat.

"Jameela, this is my nephew, Ali, from London."

A tall boy with curly hair steps out from behind his uncle. I don't know anything about Pakistani fashion, but his crisp blue shalwar kameez with silver buttons isn't like the plain beige- or tan-colored ones Baba and Uncle wear. That, along with the way he's shielding his eyes from the bright light, makes it seem like he could be posing for the cover of my mom's glossy South Asian lifestyle magazine, *Libas*. I almost want to laugh.

"Asalaamualaikum," he says to me, extending his hand like a grown-up, although he can't be much older than me. "Pleasure to meet you." Ali's accent is definitely British, and his voice is deeper than I expected it to be.

"Wa . . . waalaikum asalaam," I stammer as his dark eyes pierce mine. Suddenly I have another vision of how disheveled I must appear, and my cheeks heat up from more than the hot sun. I offer a limp handshake, try to cover up the stain on my shirt by folding it over, and gesture toward the stairs.

"Come on in. It's a lot cooler inside. Everyone's upstairs," I mumble. "I have to . . . um. I'll be right back. I just have to change and um, get ready."

2

"How do you like Atlanta, Ali?" Mama asks when we're crammed around the dining table. Everyone's plates and bowls are filled with the traditional Pakistani treats that my mother serves on Eid, along with other favorites my sisters and I have added over the years.

"It's pretty good," Ali answers politely after he polishes off his fifth or sixth samosa.

I try not to stare at how much he's eating or fixate on Ali's mouth while he speaks. I know that Desi people can have British accents and that there are tons of people who immigrated at some point from India and Pakistan living in the United Kingdom. But I haven't met any of them before, and Ali's voice doesn't seem to match his face.

There's a cupcake sitting on my plate, and I slowly unwrap it from the paper, thinking this Eid might be getting better after all. Then, as I bite into the buttery cake, a glob of toffee icing falls into my lap. It leaves a greasy smear mark on the green silk of my new outfit when I try to wipe it off. I look up, but no one noticed except for Ali, who hides his mouth behind his napkin and raises an eyebrow ever so slightly.

"Were you born in England?" Aleeza asks. She's hanging on Ali's every word and seems to have forgotten about sulking and the party we're missing as she grills him.

"Ah, yes. Born and bred."

"Why did you come here by yourself?" she presses.

Ali shifts in his seat, and I see Mama give Aleeza a signal that means "don't be nosy."

"My mum's finishing up work and selling our house. I'm here so I can begin school on time," Ali replies. He pauses for a moment before continuing. "My father died last year, and we're moving here to be near my uncle and auntie."

"Oh." Aleeza frowns and drops her head.

"We were so sorry to hear of your father's passing," Mama interjects. She reaches over the table and pats Ali's hand. "It was a huge loss for your uncle, and I know for you."

"Thank you." Ali nods, but his eyes seem darker than before.

I swallow hard, remembering when Uncle Saeed's younger brother passed away unexpectedly. Mama took massive amounts of food to their house to feed the crowds of people offering condolences. When I went over, I saw Uncle Saeed cry so intensely his shoulders shook, even though he made no sound. The image of his grief haunted me for days. It feels weird to connect that moment to Ali months later, realize I don't know any details about how or why his father died, and imagine how Ali must feel.

"I'm sorry Faisal isn't here." Uncle Saeed changes the subject and brings up my father.

"He had a meeting that couldn't be rescheduled," Mama explains.

"We understand. But how terrible for him to have to miss Eid." Auntie pours herself a piping-hot cup of tea despite the fact that she was just complaining again about the weather. It doesn't matter that we're in the South. My parents and their friends aren't ever going to switch from drinking chai to my favorite thing about living in Georgia: extra-sweet tea with lots of ice.

"We know how it is," Uncle Saeed adds. "Don't worry."

Mama's definitely worried, because her lips are pressed together like they are when she's anxious, but she doesn't say anything else to explain why Baba's meeting is important enough for him to be away. The truth is, there's no way Baba would normally let work get in the way of celebrating Eid. But a few weeks ago, the contract he was working on for over two years at the Centers for Disease Control ended without any warning. That's why he doesn't have any work right now. And that's why he flew to Maryland to explore what he called "a new opportunity."

"Do you have to go?" my sisters and I whined in a chorus when we heard the news.

"No one would schedule meetings on Christmas," I argued. "Eid is like Christmas. It's no fair!"

Baba shrugged, jokingly asked me not to write letters to the editor to protest the unfairness of his interview date, and promised to be gone only for a night.

I study my mother's face while she tries to act like everything is fine. I know it's an act, because I've overheard my parents discussing money and how we'll need to make "major changes" if Baba doesn't find a new job soon. I have no idea what those are, but Mama already took extra shifts at the physical therapy practice where she works as an office manager.

Since there's no sweet tea, I pour myself a cup of chai and take a careful sip. Bleh. It's bland.

"Can you pass the sugar?" I point to the sugar bowl in front of Ali. "Please."

"How much?" He uncovers the bowl for me.

"Three," I say.

"Jam likes tea with her sugar," Mama explains.

"Bad for your teeth." Uncle Saeed jumps at the chance to offer free dental advice. "Did you know some people hold a sugar cube in their teeth as they sip tea? Terrible idea."

Ali hesitates, not sure what to do, but I push my cup forward. He obliges me and drops three heaping spoons of sugar into my teacup.

"Thanks." As the sugar dissolves, I feel everyone watching us, and warmth fills my cheeks. It might be the steam from the tea that's making me flushed again. Or the fear of cavities after Uncle Saeed's warning. Or maybe it's the way Ali is looking at me?

"You'll be in eighth grade, right?" Mama steers the conversation back to Ali's plans. "Maryam will be starting at the high school this year. But Jameela will be at your school, in seventh grade. She can help you out."

"That's fab," Ali says.

"Don't you mean 'brilliant'?" Aleeza asks. "Isn't that what you people say?"

"Don't say 'you people,'" Bisma whispers loudly. "It's racist."

"Racist against who?" Aleeza shoots back while I roll my eyes.

"Hey, hey." Mama suppresses a laugh. "If you guys are done eating, why don't you go show Ali around?"

Maryam picks up her dishes. "Come on, Ali."

"Brilliant," Ali says. He winks at Aleeza and lifts his plate and cup, and we follow him into the kitchen.

"You're our guest." Maryam places her dishes in the sink and takes Ali's out of his hands. "You don't need to do that."

"So, this is the kitchen," Aleeza announces. She waves her hand as if she's showing off a prize on a game show.

"This is twice the size of our kitchen back home." Ali takes in the counters crammed with appliances and canisters, and then walks over to the refrigerator, which is covered with photos, magnets, and coupons.

The most recent issue of the *Mirza Memos* is tacked up on the fridge too. I write new issues to celebrate things that happen in the family, share big news, or deliver not-so-subtle messages. This one's headline screams MISSING LEFTOVER PASTA! *INVESTIGATION UNDERWAY, PERSON OF INTEREST SOUGHT*. I try to pull Ali's attention away before he notices it or the photo booth images of me making duck faces with my best friends Lily and Kayla from the school carnival last May.

"If you think this kitchen is big, you must think Uncle Saeed's house is a palace," I say.

Ali turns to face me.

"A bit, yeah. The bedrooms and closets are huge! My sister would be over the moon."

"How old's your sister?" Maryam asks.

"Zoya's three years younger than me. I'm fourteen, so that makes her . . . man, almost eleven already."

"Same as me." Bisma taps his arm and smiles shyly.

"Is that right? No wonder we're going to be mates," Ali says with a gentle smile. I feel a rush of gratitude and wonder how he already seems to see Bisma the way I do—something precious to handle with extra care.

We walk into the family room, and Ali sits on the worn, overstuffed armchair I've claimed as mine. I feel three sets of eyes on me, as my sisters probably wait for me to tell him to "move it" like I would to them. I'm tempted, but imagine my mother's warning to behave and be a good host. So I let him stay put, and settle onto the sofa to see what else we can learn about our brilliant British guest.

3

He's nice, for a boy," Bisma declares. She's wearing owl pajamas and is nestled into the pile of stuffed animals on her bed.

"Yeah." Aleeza is lying across the foot of the bed. "It'll be fun to have a brother around for a change."

That's what Mama called Ali when we said good-bye to him. Actually, she didn't exactly call him our brother. She'd given him a big hug and said, "You're going to be the son I never had." That stung a little, since I've grown up hearing elder aunties ask for years if she was going to "try for a boy." I always felt proud when she'd respond that she was perfectly happy with her girls. I decided that Mama was probably just being motherly with Ali, the way she is with my friends whenever they come over.

We sat talking in the family room with him for at least an hour and ended up missing the Eid party completely. Aleeza continued to interrogate Ali with questions like when would his mom get here (he doesn't know yet), whether he'd ever met the queen of England (not yet), and if his school was like Hogwarts (not quite). Ali quickly turned things around and started asking us about our lives, like what we do for fun, what activities we enjoy, what school's like, and so on.

While we were talking, he looked directly at each of us when we spoke about ourselves. But he dropped his eyes and twirled the tassel on the end of the pillow next to him whenever we asked about his life in London. The only thing he was excited to discuss was his favorite football team, Arsenal. It was confusing at first, until he explained that football in England is what we call soccer, and that he doesn't understand American football. I invited him to watch a Falcons game with Baba and me so we could teach him, and he acted surprised at first but quickly accepted the offer and thanked me.

I caught him staring at Maryam a few times when she wasn't paying attention, which is no shock. She has one of those faces you want to keep looking at. People gawk at her all the time, and I've gotten used to it. Mostly.

Sometimes it's hard to not feel bad that I don't have the same effect on people.

Maryam and Mama share wide eyes, high cheekbones, smooth brown skin, and thick wavy hair. I look more like my father, but with long dark wild curls, softer features, and a rounded nose. Bisma has curls like mine, only hers are a medium brown. And it looks like she's not done growing into her face, with eyes that are too large for it and a tiny nose. I'm accustomed to hearing that Aleeza is the sister whose face most resembles mine, but all I see is that we share the same scowl. She's got silky shoulder-length hair that's usually in a headband, and turquoise-framed glasses.

"I want a cupcake," Maryam says. She's scrubbed the makeup off her face and is wearing sweats, which makes her seem younger and even prettier than earlier. She picks herself up off the carpet, where she's been sitting with an extra pillow from my bed. "Anyone else want one?"

"I already brushed my teeth." I remember Uncle Saeed's warnings. "Plus, I had two."

"I'll have one." Aleeza jumps up after Maryam. That's the way it usually goes. She follows Maryam in every way, and Maryam babies her. I wonder if the two of them formed a unit because they share a room, or if it would have been that way anyway. Either way, I'm glad that as long as I have to have a roommate, I got Bisma. Apart from getting on my nerves and butting heads with me, Aleeza is incredibly messy. Her art supplies are always scattered everywhere—markers, pencils, scraps of paper, and, the worst, sequins and beads that are hidden in the carpet until I step on them in bare feet.

"No eating in our room," I yell. I'm in my favorite pair of worn cotton pajama bottoms and a free T-shirt Baba got at a conference that's been washed so many times you can hardly see the lettering on it anymore. Mama threatened to throw it away now that it has a small hole where the shoulder meets the sleeve, but it's my favorite, and I refuse to part with it.

"Are you nervous about school starting?" Bisma asks me. I'm not so much nervous as I am sad that summer is ending, but I know my sister well enough to know that *she* is.

"A little bit," I lie. "Everyone gets nervous."

"Do you know what you're going to wear?"

"Probably jeans. And this shirt."

"You can't wear that shirt! It's so ugly," Bisma giggles.

"We'll see. What about you?" Bisma's going to be in fifth grade, at the same school she's attended since kindergarten, but she gets anxious every year about her new teacher, friends, and everything else.

"Leggings and a shirt. Or maybe I should wear a dress? I don't know." Bisma bites her lip.

"We'll put together a nice outfit for you tomorrow. You have a couple days." Fashion is more Maryam's department than mine, but Bisma acts relieved anyway.

"Thanks," she says. "I hope my friends are in my class."

"Me too," I say with a yawn, and I crawl into my covers. In sixth grade Lily and I got in trouble for talking in Spanish class so often I'm afraid they're going to find a way to keep our schedules separate.

"Ali has to be alone in that big house," Bisma says at the same time that my thoughts drift back to him. I wonder what he thought of us. We managed to make him laugh a few times, especially when Aleeza started speaking in a fake British accent without realizing it. She denied it and started hitting me with a pillow when I pointed it out. Then the rest of us started saying the most absurd phrases we could come up with, like, "The queen would like some more crumpets and a spot of tea" or "Can you kindly place the rubbish in the bin" or whatever else popped into our heads while Ali corrected us. Ali had to wipe his eyes after cracking up when Aleeza joined back in and started blurting out random lines she's memorized from the Harry Potter movies.

"Ali isn't alone," I correct Bisma. "Uncle and Auntie are there too."

"Yeah, but they work so much. And his cousins live far away. Mama said he has to spend lots of time with us so he doesn't feel lonely."

Mama sticks her head in the doorway.

"That'll be okay, right? He's a good kid," she says. After a pause she adds in a lower voice, "I'm sure."

"What do you mean?" I lift my head off my pillow, and she comes into the room.

Mama sits down on the edge of Bisma's bed, and the frame squeaks. "Well, it's completely understandable, but Auntie said he had a rough time after his father died, and he got in some trouble. That's another reason why his mother sent him here, so he can get a fresh start."

I sensed there was something more when I saw Ali's expression harden and noticed how he changed the subject when we asked about his life at home.

"That's got to be so hard. What a rough age to lose a father." Mama shakes her head at the thought.

I try to imagine it and shudder under my sheet. I love my mother like crazy, and my sisters, too, but Baba's the person in our family who gets me the most. We have the exact same sense of humor and taste in movies. He's the one who encourages me to write and reviews my articles for me, and he says my passion is going to save journalism.

One Eid without Baba was hard enough, and that was with us talking to him on the phone. Twice. I don't know how Ali seems as good as he does after what he's been through.

Mama comes closer and gives me a peck on the cheek. Even in her worn robe, she is elegant and beautiful—like an older version of Maryam, with grays in her hair and lines around her eyes. Her face is wet, and there are drops of water on her forehead, which I know means she just washed up and is going to say her nightly prayers before sleeping. Mama is the one we see constantly praying in our home, and she gently reminds the rest of us that we should too. I try to, but, like Baba, I get distracted and forget sometimes.

"We'll do whatever we can to help him adjust, right?" Mama asks.

"Yeah, sure," I promise.

"I hope you had a nice Eid," Mama continues. "Even if it didn't work out the way we expected."

"It was good." I say it to be polite at first. But as I close my eyes, I mean it. It was a good one—missing Baba, skipping the party, caramel cupcakes, mysterious curly-haired boys, and all.

4

Let's see." Lily grabs my schedule sheet out of my hand as soon as she finds me in the gym.

"Anything?" I squeeze my eyes shut, afraid to see her face while she compares our classes.

"We have . . . science and English together."

"Really?" My eyes pop open.

"Wait. And gym."

"Yes! I thought for sure they'd keep us apart this year." Lily grabs my arm and does a happy dance.

"They can't keep track of all the kids who talk too much. That's almost everyone."

"True."

"Cute outfit." Lily checks me out. "But what's that? Is there *glitter* on your shirt?"

"It's Maryam's." I tug at the shirt, which is tighter than I prefer. The lettering on it has a bit of a shimmer, and I'm worried it makes me look like I'm trying too hard. "Is it weird? It was Bisma's idea."

"I like it. It's different from the dark stuff you wear." First Mama and Farah Auntie, now Lily. Everyone else is more concerned with how I dress than I am most of the time.

"I heard we do a lot of writing in English this year," Lily continues. "I hope we get to be partners."

Lily is a fantastic writer, and that's one of the reasons we became friends. Back in third grade, our teacher created an after-school writing club that we both joined. Lily wrote the most-creative fiction and decided she wanted to be an author one day. I discovered I was more interested in writing about real life. My stories ended up like newspaper articles, and that's where I got the idea to start the *Mirza Memos* and wrote the first issue. Last year, Lily heard about newspaper club before I did and pushed me to join it. Like Baba, she always cheers me on.

"There you are!" Kayla practically skips into the gym and gives us both a hug. Her black hair is twisted into two long braids, and her skin is extra tanned after a week in Hilton Head with her grandparents to end the summer.

"Let's see your schedule." I point to the green sheet in Kayla's hand. Our heads are close together as we scan the tiny print.

"Ugh. I have Señora Sherman for Spanish again," Kayla moans.

"Look!" Lily cheers. "You're in our gym class."

"And you have World Studies with me," I add. Kayla is bubbly and radiant like always. She makes everything more fun, and she and her mother have the best ideas for her birthdays. Last year her parents took us to a real stable, where we had a riding lesson, since she's obsessed with horses. It helps that her family has a lot of money, but Kayla never makes me feel bad that mine doesn't. She acted like it was completely fine when I was the only one who showed up in beat-up sneakers instead of riding boots for her party.

"What about you guys?" Kayla asks us. "Do you have other classes together?"

Lily fills Kayla in, and I search the gym for any sign of Ali, who's supposed to be starting school today too. When the crowd parts, I see dark curly hair that could be his. It is! He's taller than a lot of the other kids and is wearing a red-and-white soccer jersey. Before I look away, our eyes meet, and his face breaks into a smile. Then he starts to walk over. He doesn't know that eighth graders never venture into the seventh-grade area. Just like we avoid the section where the sixth graders are clustered.

"Salaam," Ali says when he reaches me. "I was hoping to find you."

"Salaam." I can feel my friends' stares like laser beams.

"They assigned me a 'buddy' to show me around the building today." Ali shows me a slip with a name on it. "I have no idea who this person is."

"Me neither."

"Can I see?" Kayla reads the name. "Oh, Jeremy. He's that kid over there in the green T-shirt."

"Right. Thanks. You're Jameela's friend?"

"Yeah. I'm Kayla."

"I saw your photo on Jameela's fridge." Ali grins, which means he did see the duck-face photos. "I'm Ali."

"And this is Lily." I remember my manners.

"You're British, right?" Lily asks.

"Right."

"G'day, mate," Kayla says.

The rest of us groan.

"You're doing an Australian accent." Lily pokes Kayla with her elbow.

"We say 'mate,'" Ali says. "But not the way you did."

I laugh, knowing he's probably going to hear whatever people think is British all day long. The kid named Jeremy finds us.

"Are you Ollie?" he asks Ali.

"Ah, yeah." Ali glances at me and doesn't have to say a word for me to know exactly what he's thinking.

"Cool. I'm Jeremy. I'll show you your locker and take you to your first class," Jeremy offers.

"Brilliant. G'day, maties." Ali mimics the horrible accent Kayla used. Then he addresses me directly. "See you later."

"See you. Good luck."

While he walks away, my friends turn to me and wait until he's out of earshot. Then they start squealing about how cute he is and how cool his accent is. As I hush them, I have a feeling a whole lot of people are going to feel the same way about him.

5

Ms. Levy peers over her reading glasses at me, and I begin to sweat despite the AC blasting. It's the third day of school, and I'm in my newspaper club advisor's cramped office, next to the classroom where she teaches English and runs our meetings. She asked me to come in during lunch when she passed me in the hall, but didn't say why. I don't think I can be in trouble. Newspaper club hasn't started meeting yet for the new school year.

"Now, Jameela. This isn't the norm. But I'm ready to make you . . ." Ms. Levy pauses dramatically, and I wonder what she's going to make me do. "Features editor of the *Crossing* this year!" She smiles, and I spot a dab of dark pink lipstick on her teeth.

"What?"

"I'm making you features editor. You showed strong writing skills last year, and a big commitment to the paper, and I think you'll do a great job."

"Really? I thought I was in trouble."

"No, you're not." Ms. Levy pauses. "But there is one more thing."

"Yeah?"

"I'm naming Travis editor in chief."

"Travis?"

"Travis. The job always goes to an eighth grader. He worked hard for it and is very organized and on task."

"Oh." I chew on my lip. Ms. Levy knows Travis is the reason I came close to quitting newspaper club last year. Three times. And he's the reason why I've been called into this office more than once to get a lecture from Ms. Levy.

"Jameela?" Ms. Levy taps a nail that's long and painted pink, and I think there's a unicorn drawn on it. "Do you think you two can manage to work together?"

"Um, yeah. I guess."

"That doesn't sound very convincing. I need you to be sure. I'm asking you both before I announce anything to the rest of the group. There are plenty of eighth graders who would want to be in your position."

"Did you ask *him*? Is he okay with working with *me*?"

"He's next. I'm talking to you first. You need to promise me you won't fight like last year. It created a negative environment for the staff."

"But he always acted like my ideas were dumb. And pitched the same boring articles over and over." It's true. Travis's idea of an exciting editorial was convincing people that the stop sign in front of the school should be a traffic light. He never wanted to touch real stories or issues that involved investigating, like exposing waste in the school cafeteria.

"This isn't the *AJC* or the *New York Times*, Jameela." It's like Ms. Levy is reading my mind.

"I know," I say. "But how many articles can we have about a new school mascot? It's so boring."

"It's a middle school newspaper. It's fine to focus on the issues that middle schoolers care about, and that they can relate to."

"No one cares about any of the stuff we write about now. They barely read the paper." I think of the times I fumed as I saw people toss their papers into the trash can minutes after getting them in class. Some didn't even have the decency to recycle. Maybe if we wrote about something real, they'd be more interested.

"Then be creative. But you can't force your ideas

on everyone, or get angry if they don't agree." Ms. Levy pulls her chair closer to her desk and leans in. "Listen. I know how passionate you are about writing and journalism. Being features editor is a big honor for a seventh grader."

I know that. Ms. Levy could have easily picked any of the other staff members who didn't fight with Travis instead of me.

"I admire your spunk. You remind me of me when I was younger," Ms. Levy says.

I can't imagine Ms. Levy ever being young, no matter how hard she tries with the unicorn nails and cartoon posters in her office.

"I had strong opinions too, and liked to go against the grain," she continues.

It isn't clear if those are supposed to be good things or not. I decide it's a compliment.

"This experience will prepare you well for editor in chief next year."

My heart starts to pound faster as she says the words "editor in chief." That's what I've been dreaming of, ever since I wrote my first article. I've already told Ms. Levy about my grandfather and how he was the division chief for the *Pakistan Times*, the very first English newspaper in the country. I grew up hearing stories of his bravery as a war reporter, the famous people he interviewed, and his award-winning features. I doubt he ever settled for stories that were second-rate just because they were safer, or what someone told him people wanted to read. Some of his plaques are displayed on the bookshelves in our family room—gold-and-green marble slabs engraved with his name: Mohammad Mirza. I want to be just like him one day. And I can't wait to tell Baba the news when I get home.

"And then who knows, after editor, maybe the *Washington Post* or a Pulitzer next," Ms. Levy adds.

"Maybe." I can't tell if Ms. Levy is poking fun at me or not, but I'm serious about that being a real possibility someday.

"So you're going to be okay with Travis, right?"

"Yeah. I promise. We'll be fine."

"In that case, congratulations. You are features editor."

"Thank you so much." I firmly shake Ms. Levy's hand before I leave.

This visit was way better than getting one of Ms. Levy's lectures. Although I'm only going to be able to keep my promise and stay out of trouble if Travis and I figure out how to get along. There's no way I'm letting a know-it-all eighth grader dictate what a good feature is. I'm writing about important things this year, whether he likes it or not. I want to submit a story to a national media contest for middle school and win my first award—and it can't be about school spirit. Plus, I'm going to do whatever it takes to make sure I'm first in line for editor in chief next year.

6

The chili is so spicy my nose starts to run. Baba is sweating from the spice.

"This is the best you've ever made." I congratulate him, after I blow my nose.

"They weren't lying when they named it five-alarm chili. It's got chipotle peppers, ancho chilies, and jalapeños." Baba looks satisfied as he wipes his mouth with a napkin.

"I'm dying," Aleeza gasps. She's sucking in air between her lips to try to cool her burning mouth.

Maryam and Bisma gave up on the chili after a taste, and they're eating leftover pasta, but Mama and Aleeza are powering through their bowls.

"Have a glass of milk," Baba suggests. "It'll help."

"Or more honey." Mama hands her the jar after slathering some on her cornbread. That was Maryam's contribution to the meal—moist, dense, delicious cornbread with whole corn kernels in it.

"What's this in here?" I hold up my spoon to Baba and point to an ingredient I don't recognize.

"I added some crushed tortilla chips."

"Mmm."

"Didn't the recipe have beer in it?" Mama asks. "What did you substitute?"

"Ginger ale and some chicken stock," Baba says. Since there's no alcohol in our house, my parents find creative ways around it in recipes.

"It's so good," I repeat.

"Thanks, Jam." Baba seems pleased with our reaction. It's become a tradition for him to make an enormous pot of chili for us to eat during Sunday football games every fall. He's worked through different recipes on his quest to find the best one. I'm convinced this one might be it, but he'll have to tone down the heat a little so everyone can enjoy it.

Sundays during football season are one of the rare occasions when we're allowed to turn on the TV during dinner. Even though it's preseason, we're watching the Falcons dominate the Buccaneers in the third quarter.

The Falcons have the ball and are driving toward the end zone again.

"I don't know how you watch this." Mama winces during a tackle that's so hard we hear a loud cracking sound before the whistle. "It's so brutal."

"It's got issues," Baba agrees. "But I still love it."

Baba told me that he discovered football when he moved to Ohio from Pakistan during high school and didn't have any friends. He said learning everything he could about the game helped him fit in and feel like he could be as American as everyone else. Today, apart from the slightest accent when he pronounces the letter *v* like a *w*, you'd think he grew up in Columbus, not Islamabad. I'm always impressed by how Baba can talk to people he's just met about football, news, or the weather, and make them instantly feel like an old friend. Aleeza's more like him in that way than I am, and I'm more like Mama, friendly but careful around people I don't know.

What I like most about watching the games is that they've been my special time with Baba over the years. When I was younger, he taught me to throw a football in this very room with a small blue Nerf ball and bragged to his friends about my perfect spiral.

"Football should be banned," Mama declares, like

she's personally responsible for the safety of all the players. "These kids start playing when they're too young to understand the consequences."

"There's an article for you, Jam," Baba suggests. "Try polling kids at school about banning football as a sport and see what they say."

That's not a bad idea. A lot of the boys at school wear football jerseys and can't wait to get to high school to play, since we don't have a middle school team. I'm sure others would argue against it. It could be a debate.

"Maybe." I smile at Baba. "Thanks for the idea."

When I told him my news about becoming features editor a few days ago, my father's face lit up, and he broke into his goofy dad dance—the same one he does after touchdowns. It's an extremely bad version of the running man, but I jumped up and joined him, and we danced until we were out of breath.

Everyone else was happy for me too. Mama squeezed me in a gigantic hug, Maryam baked me brownies, and Aleeza presented me with a sticker that says "Looking Good" with the one-eyed monster from *Monsters, Inc.* on it that she got from the doctor's office. Bisma said that I should write an article about myself becoming features editor for the school paper, which made us laugh. I doubt Travis would go for that.

"I need something sweet," Mama says. "Who wants to go to Publix with me to get ice cream?"

"Mint chocolate chip!" Maryam suggests.

"Cookies and cream," I add.

"Can we go out to Yogurtland instead?" Aleeza asks.

Mama and Baba exchange a look, and then Mama says, "That'll cost a lot more. Let's do that another time, okay?"

"I'll go with you," Bisma offers, which is good, since I'm not leaving before the game is over but want Mama to get the right flavors. I can imagine her coming home with butter pecan and saying, "Isn't that what you said you wanted?" She can be absentminded like that, but Bisma will remember what everyone wants.

Maryam starts to clear the dishes, but Baba and I hold on to our bowls and take another helping of chili.

"Crumble some cornbread into it." Baba hands me the last piece. "It's even better that way."

He's right. The cornbread cuts the spice level down to perfect. But I'm still thinking about what Mama said about the frozen yogurt. When I walked into the kitchen after breakfast this morning, Mama and Baba were talking quietly. I wasn't trying to eavesdrop, but I heard Mama say she was worried about the house payment and Baba tell her to try to relax and that everything would work out. Mama had started to respond when she heard me come in, and looked up in surprise.

"What are you doing?" Mama quickly tried to relax her face into a smile.

"Nothing," I said, acting like I hadn't heard anything. "Just wanted some water."

"That filter needs to be changed. Take some from the pitcher." Baba got up and handed me a glass.

I could tell neither of them wanted me to stick around, so I left with my water and a swarm of questions buzzing around in my brain. The biggest one was, what will happen if Baba doesn't get a job soon?

"Yes!" Baba shouts as the Falcons get a rushing touchdown. He slaps me a high five as I finish my last bite.

"Chili, football, family. This is what a Sunday should be," he says.

"And ice cream," Aleeza adds.

"And ice cream. How could I forget?"

I study Baba's face, and he doesn't look stressed out about work, money, or anything else. So I sit back and try to enjoy the rest of the game.

7

"What do you guys want to do?" I ask.

"Play something?" Bisma suggests from the red-leather chair behind the desk. She picks up a glass paperweight and places it over her eye, magnifying it until it's huge.

Aleeza pulls a book off the shelf and holds it up for us to see. It's called *Would You Rather . . . ? Radically Repulsive* and must have belonged to Samir, Uncle Saeed's youngest son, who lives in Chicago now. Uncle has stories about how he loved everything disgusting as a kid and played the best practical jokes on his older sister.

"Let's play this," she says.

We're sitting in the den in Uncle Saeed's house, its shelves stuffed with books and games like Connect 4, an old version of Monopoly, Scrabble, and Clue. There's a beat-up leather couch, an old exercise bike, and a large desk with brass drawer pulls.

"How do you play a book?" Bisma asks.

"We'll take turns asking each other the questions," Aleeza says. "I'll go first. So, Ali . . ." She pauses to flip through the book and then reads: "'Would you rather . . . have your face repeatedly paddled for five minutes by Ping-Pong world champions OR have someone do the 'got your nose' trick and really rip off your nose?'"

Ali shrugs. "What's the got-your-nose trick?"

"You don't have that in England? I'll show you." Aleeza walk over to Ali, who's sitting on the exercise bike. She tries and fails miserably at pretending to pull off his nose.

"See, here's your nose." She shows him her bent thumb, which is clearly still attached to her hand and not fooling anyone into thinking it's part of his face.

"I'd go for the face paddling for sure. Do I get to demonstrate that now?" Ali holds out his hand.

"No!" Aleeza jumps back, squealing. "Now you ask one."

Ali thumbs through the book until he finds a page he likes. "All right, so . . . ah . . . Maryam. 'Would you rather . . . have an hour-long chat with your five-year-old self OR with your forty-year-old self?'"

"I don't know." Maryam ponders the question and gets lost in thought.

"Come on, any day now," I nudge.

"That's so hard. I'm around a five-year-old when I babysit, and he says the funniest things. I loved to talk to myself when I was that age. But I think I'd rather meet my forty-year-old self. I want to see what I'll look like. And maybe ask her what kind of advice she would give my current self."

"Do you think you would listen to anything your old self had to say?" I ask while Ali slowly pedals the exercise bike. It makes a squeaking sound with each rotation.

"Probably not."

"Your turn." Ali waves the book at Maryam, who has her face in her phone now and is frowning at the screen.

"Okay." Maryam grabs the book. "Everyone, would you rather go to the movies with your friends on a Friday night to kick off the weekend or play a silly game at your uncle's house with your siblings?"

"Hey! That's not nice!" Aleeza complains. "That's not what it says."

"Fine," Maryam says, conceding, and she puts her

phone back in her pocket. "I'm kidding. But my friends are at the movies, and I'm stuck here."

"Are you suggesting we're not as fun as your friends?" Ali acts indignant. "I'm . . . offended."

"No, but everyone is hanging out, and I'm seeing it on Instagram. It looks like they're having a blast.

"I miss everything my friends are doing all the time," Ali says.

"That's why social media is messed up. It makes you worry about what you're *not* doing, or lets everyone else know what *they're* not doing. And then you can't enjoy what you're doing now," I say.

"Ah, hello. Is this Jameela, or her forty-year-old self?" Ali asks me.

"Maybe both," I admit. I do sound like a mom.

"Can we play a regular game now?" Bisma suggests. "How about Pictionary?"

Aleeza claps her hand at that idea. She's great at drawing, while the rest of us sisters can barely make a stick figure. But Baba pops his head into the doorway right then.

"You guys ready to go?"

"Can we stay longer?" Aleeza begs.

Baba comes into the den and surveys us, scattered around the room in our various poses. "Fifteen more minutes."

He gives Ali a pat on the shoulder on the way out. Baba only met Ali today for the first time, since he was away on Eid, but you'd never know it. They seem like old buddies already.

"Wait, Baba." Bisma stops him before he leaves. "'Would you rather . . . have to wear the same underwear for two weeks straight OR have to wear the same pair of socks for two months straight?'"

Baba scratches his head, like he's seriously pondering the question.

"That's a tough one. I can't choose. I'm already doing both."

"Ewww!" Bisma giggles as Baba bows and exits the room.

We spend the next hour playing a hilarious new game that Ali makes up: Pictionary: the Would You Rather version. Maryam gets totally into it and yells the loudest, and she leaves her phone in her pocket until my parents finally round us up to go home.

8

"Who is Abu Dhabi?" Aleeza clutches Baba's arm and presses closer to him on the sofa.

Baba smiles.

"It's a country," Mama explains. "Well, an emirate."

"A what?"

"It's one of the United Arab Emirates. So kind of like the United States. But with royalty."

"Arab?" Aleeza looks skeptical. "How far away is it?"

"Far." Baba's voice is low. "As far as Pakistan."

Aleeza's eyes bug out from behind her glasses.

"How long do you have to go for?" Bisma asks from the other side of our father.

"Only for a few months, until I find something else

here." Baba puts his arm around Bisma and pats her shoulder.

"How many months?" I ask.

"At least six," Baba sighs.

My stomach clenches like I'm bracing for a punch, and everyone sits in stunned silence as we process that information.

Aleeza's eyes well up, and her lip starts to quiver. "So we won't be able to see you for six whole months?" she asks.

"I'll come home to visit during that time. And I'll talk to you every day. We'll video chat."

"But you'll be alone there." Bisma frowns as she imagines what it will be like for our father. "What will you do by yourself?"

"Get bored. And probably watch a lot of movies. I'll manage." Baba tries to reassure us, but I can tell he's not any happier about this development than we are.

It was obvious that something strange was going on the minute he said he wanted to sit down and talk to us before dinner on a Tuesday night. The way he and Mama were speaking to each other in Urdu like they do when they don't want us to understand, I knew it was going to be something big. But I had no idea it would be this big.

"Why can't you do the job from here?" Aleeza sniffles. "You work from home sometimes, don't you?"

"Yes, but I need to be at the client site for this contract."

"Will you have to learn Arabic, then?" Maryam asks. "Why can't they get someone who lives there already?"

"It's an international company, and everyone speaks English. The team is coming from different countries, including here," Baba says.

"But I don't want you to go." Aleeza scowls. "Just say you won't do it."

Baba clears his throat and turns to Mama for help.

"Come on," Mama jumps in. "We'll have lots of girl time. And this is only for a little while, right?"

"Six months isn't a little while!" Aleeza argues.

"Well, it'll go by before we know it. Come on, girls. This is a great opportunity for Baba and a big deal for him to win this contract. It'll be good for us, inshallah."

She doesn't sound completely convinced herself, and I'm pretty sure my sisters see that as clearly as I do. But I wonder if this means she won't have to worry about paying the bills anymore.

"Will you make a lot of money?" I ask.

"Jam!" Mama looks annoyed. "What kind of question is that?"

"It's okay," Baba chuckles. "It's good money. A little extra for a few months will be helpful. But I need you to behave when I'm not here and help Mama out." Baba is saying this to the four of us, but he's focusing on Aleeza. She wipes her nose on her sleeve and blinks back tears.

"When do you have to leave?" I ask.

"Next week."

"Next week?" I sputter.

"So soon?" Maryam adds.

Baba doesn't speak, and his face is so sad I don't want to make it worse. I swallow hard, determined not to cry. This is really happening! Eid was tough enough without our father, and that trip was only for a night. Now we won't have him at home for at least six months, if not longer. The idea of him being on the other side of the world, in a place I know nothing about, scares me.

"But you're the one who takes me to swimming lessons," Aleeza says. "Who's going to take me?"

"I'll figure it out," Mama interjects. "Or we can find a carpool."

"I wish I was old enough to drive. That would help," Maryam says.

"No it wouldn't," Aleeza snorts. "I'm never getting into a car that you're driving."

"Me neither," I agree. This time I'm completely with

Aleeza. "Remember how you almost ran over that old lady with your bike? Imagine if it was a car."

"I missed her by at least a foot!"

"What about the time you got lost walking home from school?" Baba adds. "You have no sense of direction."

"I was only in fourth grade! And I wasn't paying attention," Maryam protests.

"I was so frightened when you didn't come home. I drove around the whole neighborhood and found you happily playing with a cat six blocks from here." Mama is amused now, but she was furious then. The only time we see Mama get angry like that is when she's worried about us.

"Can we get a cat to keep us company while you're away?" Aleeza turns to Baba and uses her most wheedling tone. Trust her to think of a way to manipulate this situation to get something she wants. "Or a dog! Mrs. Gupta got a Goldendoodle puppy, and he's so cute!" she adds.

"I don't think so." Mama shakes her head. "It's another responsibility and expense we don't need right now."

"Pleeeeease!" Aleeza isn't about to let this go easily.

"Let's talk about it later," Baba says. Aleeza clasps her hands together in excitement, but I know it's futile to dream of a dog. Or a gerbil. Or even a goldfish.

Baba works on preventing infectious disease, and he's

obsessed with germs and washing hands. When Maryam and I were little, we begged for a pet more than once, but every time we got a lecture on the different risks each one brought. I was the only kid in preschool who used the word "feces," because Baba talked about the dangers that lurk in various animals' poop. Gross. I've given up on having a pet, unless you count the lizards in the garage.

Now Baba's going to travel all the way to the Middle East to help set up the infectious disease department of a new hospital. It does sound like a big deal, and it's great that he'll make more money, but what if he ends up staying longer? What if we have to move out there too? And I end up going to a new school? What about my friends? I'd lose my spot on the newspaper! My mind starts to race with the possibilities.

"Aren't you guys hungry? Let's eat." Baba interrupts my thoughts and changes the subject. "Is there any left-over chili?"

I suddenly realize that he's not going to be here to watch the regular season with me, even though the Falcons have playoff hopes. I can't imagine what that is going to be like, or how empty the house will feel without him. I'd easily pick a losing record and give up the postseason if it meant I could keep my father home with us, where he belongs.

9

Ali is sprawled out facedown on the carpet.

"Ohhh," he moans. "I ate too much. Your mum's cooking is so good."

"What about yours?" Bisma asks. "Aren't all *mums* good cooks?"

"She's all right." Ali sits up with panic on his face. "But don't ever tell her that! Please. She would be gutted."

"You can trust us," I promise. "Mama was crushed when I said Farah Auntie's turkey was better than hers last Thanksgiving. It was literally the first time I ever said that something she made wasn't the best. I learned my lesson."

"I do miss my mum's porridge in the mornings," Ali sighs. "I can't make it the way she does."

"Porridge? That's really a thing?" I ask.

"Nearly sure I wasn't imagining it."

"What does it taste like?" I don't want to admit I've only heard of porridge in fairy tales and *Oliver Twist*. I picture it to be gray, pasty, and completely nasty.

"You don't eat porridge? You cook cereal with water and cream. Mum adds the perfect amount of brown sugar."

"It's oatmeal, genius." Maryam is doing her homework at the dining table like usual, her hair falling over the pages of her book. She's not wearing her headphones for a change and is apparently listening to our conversation while she works.

"Oh." I point an accusing finger at Ali. "You knew that, didn't you?"

"Maybe." He smiles out of one side of his mouth. Bisma giggles from where she's sitting next to me.

"When do you think your mom will come to America?" Maryam asks, giving us her full attention now.

"I don't know. This morning she said she probably has at least a few weeks to go."

My sisters and I fall silent. We're still digesting the news of Baba being away from us, and here's Ali, pretty much alone in a foreign country. He came over for lunch today with Uncle Saeed and Farah Auntie, so they could spend some time with Baba before he leaves. After we ate, the grown-ups left for Costco together, since Uncle Saeed has a membership and Baba needs jumbo-size suitcases. Aleeza went along too. Ever since Baba shared the news of his move, she's been glued to his side. I'm pretty sure she's also hoping to score snacks for her school lunches.

"Let's go." Ali peels himself off the floor and stands up. "It's nice out. And I need to move around."

"It's too hot," I complain. Bisma checks the temperature on Mama's iPad.

"Eighty-seven degrees," she shares.

"Come on. It's not that bad. Right, Bisma? A bit of sun is good for you. You Americans spend too much time indoors."

"Fine," I grumble. "But I'm pretty sure you're not allowed to say 'you Americans.'" Ali smirks at me as I get out of my chair, which he's now figured out is mine and avoids. Or maybe someone told him.

"You coming, Maryam?" I ask, but already know the answer.

"Too much homework," she mumbles as she puts her headphones back on. Maryam used to be a decent athlete and ran track in middle school, but lately she's absorbed with school and friends, babysitting the kids who live in the apartments nearby, and experimenting with makeup. When we're lucky, she bakes something or hangs out with us.

"I'm coming." Bisma runs downstairs to put on her shoes.

"Do you have a football?" Ali asks as we head down the stairs behind her.

"I think so." I try to remember where the balls are in the garage. Ali's right about us being indoors a lot. I can't remember the last time I played in the field across from our complex. "It might take a minute."

Ali pokes through the shelves with Bisma as I rummage through a box.

"Found it!" I hold up an old Nerf football with a few tiny holes in it. It's the ball I learned to play with.

"That's not a football. Footballs are round." Ali shakes his head.

I toss it at him anyway, and it bounces off his shoulder.

"Ow." Ali rubs where I hit him. "Nice throw."

"Want me to show you how to play real football?" I offer.

"American football? Nah. But I can show *you* how to play football like the rest of the world."

"Who said I don't know how? I was on a soccer

team." It was only for one season when I was in fifth grade. And we lost every game. But I don't mention that.

"How about you, Bisma?" Ali asks.

"I played in first and second grade. I'm not that good."

"I don't believe that," Ali says.

I find my old red soccer ball behind a dusty bottle of washer fluid, and it's mushy.

"Here you go." I hand it to Ali, who inspects the ball.

"You could do with some air," he says.

Bisma somehow managed to find a pump with a needle attached while I was searching for the ball. Ali fills it until it's firm, wipes it off on his shirt like he's cleaning an apple, and holds it up. "Perfect. Let's go."

I'm starting to sweat from being in the garage, and when we open the door, the sunlight is fierce. Ali doesn't seem to care, and there's a bounce in his step as we walk across the street to the small grassy area.

"Let's kick-start."

Kick-start? Bisma and I exchange a panicked look, and I wonder if he's planning to run actual drills. I sure hope not.

10

Ali walks about ten paces away from us and kicks the ball in my direction. I stop it easily, since it basically hits my foot.

"Nice one." Ali looks impressed.

I feel good and kick it over to Bisma. Way too hard. The ball goes flying past her and into the street.

"Sorry!" I yell as she darts after it.

"Try using the inside of your foot instead of your toes," Ali suggests to me after Bisma throws the ball back in my direction. Her face is already turning red from the heat, and we only left the house ten minutes ago.

We pass the ball back and forth in silence for a couple of minutes. Bisma runs around getting the ball whenever we miss, and soon she's out of breath and sweaty. She kicks the ball hard toward Ali, and it flies up in a nice arc.

"Bob's your uncle!" Ali traps the ball with his foot.

"What?" Bisma laughs.

"It's like when you say 'way to go'!" Ali changes his voice to imitate an American accent and ends up sounding like a cowboy.

"I like 'Bob's your uncle' better," I say.

"Me too," Bisma agrees. "It's funny. Jam calls Baba 'Bobs' sometimes for short."

"Jam. Bobs. Who else in the family gets shortened?" Ali asks.

"Maryam is Murr sometimes. And that's it."

"What about you?"

"I'm always Bisma."

"That's because you're perfect the way you are," Ali says.

I can't tell if Bisma's cheeks are turning redder from the flattery or from the heat.

"Thank you. But it's too hot," Bisma pants. "Can we stop?"

"Come on, mate," Ali says. "Don't kill it."

"Sorry. I need water." Bisma squints in my direction and wipes her brow with the sleeve of her T-shirt. "I'm going in."

"You'll stay?" Ali asks me.

"For a little longer," I agree as Bisma walks back to the house.

We return to kicking the ball back and forth. After a moment, I ask Ali, "Do you play on a team?"

"Did."

"That's what I mean. Did you like it?"

"Yeah. But I quit. Or got kicked off. Not sure which." Ali passes the ball to me while he's got his back turned, and it still reaches me.

"Good one," I say as I punt it back. "Why?"

"After my dad . . . you know . . . I started working at a shop to help out with money. I missed too many practices, and Coach and I got into a fight."

"Seriously?"

"Yeah."

"Like a punching fight?" I find that hard to believe.

"No. But I swore at him."

"Why?" I stop the ball when it heads my way and don't kick it back this time.

"He insulted my mum. So I said some stuff, grabbed my things, and left. Never went back."

"What did he say?"

"Ignorant things, like how my dad probably took care of everything because of the way women from "your part of the world" are. He'd met my mum before, but assumed she didn't work, although she has a great job."

"Did you tell anyone what he said?"

"Nah. There was more than that. But it wouldn't have mattered. And the thing is, I don't think he was trying to be insulting. He was only saying what a lot of people think."

I've heard my parents talk about how some of their family members in England have faced prejudice, and I want to ask more, but Ali doesn't seem eager to discuss it.

"Do you miss it? Playing soccer?" I pick up the ball and toss it back.

Ali catches it and starts to juggle the ball with his feet. He doesn't let it touch the ground. It bounces from his foot to his knee, off his chest, and back to his foot.

"I. Miss. Lots. Of. Things. About. Home. Especially. My. Sister." Ali says one word with each bounce. If I didn't know better, I would think he was moving in slow motion. He's that good.

"Your turn." He kicks it back out to me. I'm not prepared, and the ball flies off my leg.

"Sorry," he says.

"You're so good at soccer . . . I mean football," I say, instead of asking him more questions about what kind of trouble he got into and what else he misses about his life in London. I don't know much about it, only the little glimpses that Ali offers.

"You should join a team here," I continue when he doesn't respond. "The one at school is pretty decent, and there are a bunch of leagues here. I'm sure they'd want someone like you."

"I don't know."

Ali bounces the ball off his feet at least twenty times in a row.

"I mean it," I add. "I've never seen anyone play like you before."

"I try. You should see some of my mates." Ali stops playing and picks up the ball again. He seems deflated, like the soccer ball before he pumped it up. Then he turns and starts to walk back to the house. I said something wrong but don't know what it is.

"Let's get some water," he finally calls over his shoulder.

I don't get it. Why wouldn't Ali want to play a sport that he's so good at? I want to probe him, but when he doesn't want to talk about something, it feels like Ali puts up a wall that the best soccer defenders would only dream of—one that seems impenetrable. The reporter in me decides to find out the answers, one way or another. But for now I follow Ali back into the house.

11

I search for the ice cream as Ali leans against the counter in the kitchen, chugging water. We passed Bisma on the way to the kitchen. She was lying on the sofa watching TV, looking less overheated than earlier.

"Cookies and cream?" I offer.

"I seriously thought I'd never eat again before we went outside, but yes, please," Ali says.

He sounds upbeat again, so I don't bring up soccer as I dish out the ice cream into two bowls.

"What do you think of our school?" I ask instead.

"It's okay."

"I saw you hanging with Braden and Eli. Are you guys friends?"

"Maybe a tad."

"Do you like your classes?"

"They're pretty boring. Every class feels like review. Except for science. Mrs. Kilbourn is a killer."

"Maryam had her last year. She said the same thing. You should talk to her."

"I could." Ali pauses. "But . . ."

"I know. Don't worry. She's smarter than she looks."

"It's not that." Ali shakes his head. "It's just that . . ."

"What?"

"Maryam's so pretty I find it a bit distracting."

"Oh."

"I get tongue twisted when she's around," he continues with a nervous laugh.

As I swallow a spoonful of ice cream, Ali's confession hits me like brain freeze. He clearly isn't having any trouble getting his words out while he's looking at me.

"Back from the great outdoors so soon?" Maryam walks into the kitchen. She's been at home studying all day but still looks put together in a cute denim shirtdress with leggings and freshly glossed lips. I've got sweatpants and a T-shirt on, and my hair's in a ponytail that feels super frizzed out from the humidity.

"Yeah," Ali replies, and shifts his weight. I can't help but watch him, to see if he acts weird or starts to garble his words.

"Is there any more ice cream?" Maryam asks.

"In the freezer," I say.

"For real? You put this much back?" Maryam holds up the container, which has about three bites left in it. And then she goes to the drawer and pulls out a spoon.

"Saved it for you." I shrug while Maryam finishes it off. "We were talking about Mrs. Kilbourn."

"She's the worst!" Maryam groans. "You have her, Ali?"

"Yeah." Ali puts his bowl in the sink.

"You have to go in and ask for help during lunch. She wants to see that you care. It makes a huge difference."

"That's not fair," I say. "What if you have club meetings, or want to hang out with your friends. Or eat?"

"You're right—it's not fair." Maryam shakes her head. "You better hope you don't get her next year, or you might not get to newspaper."

Ms. Levy has newspaper club meetings in her classroom once a week, and she lets us eat our lunches in there as long as we don't spill or leave crumbs.

"I'd rather get a C than give up newspaper," I say.

Maryam raises her eyebrows. She's not buying it. I never get Cs.

Ali turns to me as Bisma joins us in the kitchen.

"What do you do for the school newspaper? They still have those?"

"Very funny. I'm features editor this year."

"Impressive. But . . . is it an actual paper? Like on paper?"

"Yeah."

"Hmm."

"What?"

"I'm surprised you haven't gone digital."

"Ms. Levy says the printed word is tradition. And your brain remembers what you read on paper more than on a screen."

"Maybe. But aren't traditional newspapers disappearing?"

"Some. But they shouldn't be!" I feel myself warming up again as I think about it. "Baba says it's destroying our country that people don't have attention spans anymore to read real analysis or well-researched articles, and that they want their news in a tweet instead. And Ms. Levy says—"

"What about what *you* say?" Ali interrupts me. "If you had urgent news you needed to share, would you go to a newspaper that'll be printed the next day or the next week? Or would you go to social media?"

"I'm not allowed on social media."

"Really?"

"Yeah. Maryam finally got Instagram this summer. My parents said not until we're in high school."

"If my friends back home didn't follow me, they'd have no idea what I'm doing. Like right now." Ali aims his phone at me, and I duck, while Maryam starts checking her hair and Bisma poses.

"No pictures!" I protest and put a hand in front of my face. "And what I say is that social media does *not* take the place of real journalism. Just because something is faster doesn't make it better! And you can get information that is flat-out lies that anyone makes up, or one side of a story and—"

"Relax, Jam," Maryam cuts me off right when I start to get going. "Ali's entitled to his opinion. We don't need to have a debate."

She turns to Ali and motions for him to stand down. I'm hoping the fact that she's looking at him will make him tongue-tied. Instead he goes to the fridge and pulls off the latest issue of the *Mirza Memos* that's still there and starts to flip through it.

"Now *this*. This is journalism at its finest. We need more stories like this one." He points to a photo of Bisma on the stage at the Unitarian church during her last piano recital, beaming next to her teacher, Miss Jasmin.

"That you?" he asks Bisma. "Wicked."

"Go ahead—make fun of it." I snatch the pages out of his hand and stick them back onto the fridge with a free magnet from a real estate agent with big blond hair.

"Serious." Ali turns the page again, this time without removing it. "This is fab. Interviews, comics."

"Aleeza does the comics," Bisma volunteers.

"I wish my family had something like this." Ali's voice is softer now, and I can't tell if he's mocking my family paper, or trying to compliment me.

Everyone gets back from Costco, and there's a commotion as Ali brings up the new suitcases and Aleeza lugs a massive box of pretzel snack mix into the kitchen. Ali gives us a quick good-bye, because Uncle and Auntie are waiting for him downstairs. I straighten the newspaper on the fridge as he leaves.

I was crushed when our local newspaper went out of business recently, since I'd been hoping to write for them in high school. The school newspaper is what I have for now until I get to work for a real publication, whether it's digital or paper. And newspapers *will* be around forever, even if social media isn't. They have to be. Baba says the free press is one of the most important aspects of America. I agree with him and want to be a part of it. In the meantime, I need the *Crossing* to get me one step closer to my dreams.

12

I promised myself I wasn't going to cry and make things harder for Baba, because it's been a sob fest all day thanks to my sisters. Now that Baba is packed and ready to head to the airport, I'm having a hard time keeping it together. I haven't been away from my father for longer than a few days my entire life. Only a week after we heard the news, he's going to be living on the other side of the world for six months or longer.

Mama decided she's going to the airport alone to drop him off, rather than have us tag along. She said it was because there wasn't enough room for everyone in the minivan, along with Baba's suitcases, so someone would have had to stay home. And no one was going to volunteer. I think she also didn't want to have to deal with a big emotional scene at the security checkpoint. It's been bad enough at home.

"Let's get these loaded," Baba calls from the foyer. "Jam, give me a hand."

We walk outside to the van and open up the back. He lifts the handle of one of the suitcases, and I push from the bottom to get it inside. We hoist the second bag on top. I'm out of breath by the time we're done.

Baba checks the pockets of his shirt for his passport and ticket and phone for the seventh time. Then he rifles through his carry-on bag to make sure he has everything he needs for the long plane ride.

"Do you have your chargers?" Mama asks. "And your allergy meds?"

"Check," Baba says.

"Your banana bread?" Maryam adds. She made him a batch with peanut butter chips to eat on the plane.

"Check."

"And did you download your playlists?" Bisma put together a bunch of our favorite songs for Baba.

"Check."

"What about my drawing?" Aleeza asks. She made him a card with her signature drawing of our family, standing in a line from eldest to youngest.

"Ready to hang on my fridge when I get there," Baba

says. It occurs to me that I don't have anything to give Baba in this moment, and that I hadn't considered it. I could have put together a special farewell issue of the *Mirza Memos*. He would have loved it, no matter how difficult it might have been to write.

Baba puts his carry-on bag on the backseat and then turns around and faces us huddled together by the van. He looks exhausted even though he hasn't started traveling yet.

"I'm going to miss you so much. I can't believe I have to be so far away from you," he says.

It seems like he doesn't want the words to come out, but the fact that he's finally being real makes me feel better. For the past week, whenever anyone said anything about him leaving, Baba acted weirdly upbeat and went on about how everything was going to be fine. It put the pressure on the rest of us to pretend to be okay.

"We're going to miss you too." I swallow the lump in my throat and try not to think about the things Baba's not going to be here for over the next few months. Like Aleeza's birthday. And like my first issue of the paper. It won't be the same if I can't celebrate it with him. Baba always gets super excited and makes it a big deal when I come home with a new issue. He reads my articles aloud in an extra-deep voice like he's a newscaster.

"Your dada would be proud" are usually his final words, before his eyes fall on the bookshelves, where there are a few framed photos of my grandfather and famous people I don't recognize shaking hands or posing together.

Although I don't have a gift to give him today, I decide I'm going to write the best article Baba has ever read for my first issue and mail him a card with a clipping of it. It'll be something meaningful, important, and worthy of his praise. I'm going to make him prouder than he's ever been of me.

I reach out and give him a good-bye hug first. Baba's shirt smells like his cologne, which is usually the most comforting scent I know. Right now it makes the tears I've been holding in for hours start to flow.

Baba pats me on the back and kisses the top of my head as I let myself cry on his chest. I finally pull back and wipe my nose on the back of my hand.

"That's disgusting," Baba says. And we both laugh.

"You'll keep me posted on family news so I'm not missing anything, right?" he adds.

"I will." I don't say it, but I resolve to give him more than that.

Baba takes turns hugging everyone and finally has to peel Aleeza and Bisma off him as they cling tightly to his waist. No one says much more before he and Mama get in the minivan, but I'm certain we all feel the heaviness in the air. It's not just the hazy, hot, humid weather typical of this time of day. It's like our sadness has been released into the atmosphere, where it's pressing down on me, filling my insides, and squeezing my heart until it hurts.

"Bye, girls. Be good," Mama says to us. She quickly wipes her eyes before continuing. "There's leftover chicken in the fridge. And some salad. Eat dinner without me, because I won't be back for a few hours."

"We'll be fine," Maryam says as she gives Mama a hug. "Don't worry about us." Not only do they resemble each other, I've always felt Maryam might secretly be Mama's favorite, though she would never admit it. Mama leans on Maryam more than the rest of us, maybe because she's the eldest. And I have to admit Maryam is the most helpful of us. But they also seem to understand each other best. I wonder if my sisters would say the same thing about Baba, and my being his favorite. In this moment, I kind of hope so.

Watching the van back out of the tiny driveway, we stand close together and wave until it's out of sight. Baba's lips are pursed together like Mama's while he waves back at us.

"This feels so weird." Bisma's holding on to my hand tight, as if to make sure I'm not going to vanish.

"I know."

"Let's go inside. You guys hungry?" Maryam switches into mom mode, like she always does when she's left in charge. Right now I don't mind.

"Yeah," I say.

"Me too," Bisma adds.

"I don't feel like eating chicken again," Aleeza complains.

"I can make mac and cheese," Maryam offers. "You want that?"

"The one with shells." Aleeza claps. "I'll help." She already looks happier, though her face is blotchy. I wish pasta were enough to do it for me.

As I walk back into the house, it's hard to imagine that Baba isn't coming back in a few hours, since his presence is everywhere. His Falcons cap is lying on the console like he's about to use it, since it's his go-to hat on the weekends. Baba's bearded face smiles at me from the gallery of photos in the hallway. And his piles of books and medical journals and his collection of old-fashioned radios are scattered around the family room.

I think of Ali and his little sister having to come to terms with their father never coming home, and tears flood my eyes again. I wonder if Ali had a chance to say good-bye, and how he was able to cope with the shock. But I don't know if he will ever want to talk about his loss or grief, or about anything else that truly matters to him. Either way, I'm amazed that he finds the strength to go through life after losing someone he loved so much. And I hope I never have to know what that feels like.

13

That's my new shirt." I hear the exasperation in Bisma's voice despite her whispering. "I didn't get to wear it yet."

"You're supposed to share," Aleeza retorts. She doesn't bother to keep her volume down, although I'm in bed, and this conversation is happening in the hallway right outside my bedroom door, which is ajar. I roll over and squint at the clock. It's 6:48 a.m., and my alarm hasn't gone off yet.

"Can't I wear my own shirt before you ruin it?" Bisma says. "Last time you borrowed my white jeans you spilled tomato sauce on them. The stain never came out."

"That's because you bumped into my elbow when I was eating."

"So it's my fault you ruined my pants?"

"Kind of."

"Well I don't want you to wear my shirt."

"But I'm already wearing it!"

"Then take it off," I growl from my bed. "You can't steal Bisma's things without asking."

"You always take her side!" Aleeza cries. "It's not fair!"

"She doesn't do that with your stuff. Take it off!"

"No!"

"If I have to get up . . . ," I threaten, although I don't know what I would do if I did get up.

"You can't make me!" Aleeza shrieks and runs away when I throw off my covers in a show of rising.

"Why are you scaring her?" Maryam appears in the doorway a minute later.

"She's bullying Bisma. And taking her stuff."

"It's a shirt, Jam. They share clothes."

"But it's new, and it's not fair. Aleeza should ask before putting it on!"

"You shouldn't take sides." Maryam shrugs likes it's no big deal.

"But YOU'RE taking sides!" I yell. I like to wake up from my alarm and hit snooze three times. And when I get woken up like this, it puts me in a bad mood, fast.

"You always take Aleeza's side. That's part of the reason why she's such a brat." As I spit out the last word, I see Aleeza jump from behind Maryam like she's startled. Her eyes fill up, and she starts to wail before running toward our parents' room.

"Great. See what you did." Maryam acts like it's my fault, and not Aleeza's.

"It's too early for this." I pull my covers over my head and fume underneath until I hear Maryam go back to her room. Bisma quickly gets ready in silence. It's only when everyone finally goes downstairs for breakfast that my breathing slows back to normal.

"Jam?" I hear my mother's voice and feel her sit on the edge of my bed. The mattress tilts, and I kind of roll against her from under the covers.

"Mmmh," I grunt.

"You okay?"

"Yeah."

"Aren't you going to get ready for school?"

"Yeah."

"Can you look at me, please?"

I pull the blanket off my head. Mama's got dark circles under her eyes, and I remember her saying yesterday that she hasn't been able to sleep properly since Baba left last week.

"There you are. What's going on? Why are you screaming at your sisters first thing in the morning?"

"I was sleeping! They're the ones fighting and being loud."

"And Aleeza? Did you call her names?"

"I called her a brat. It's not a name. It's a fact. She is one. You have to admit it."

Mama's frowning, but her eyes have the hint of a smile.

"I'm not admitting anything. The last thing I need is for you to use that against her."

"See? It *is* a fact."

"Be kind, Jam. It's not easy being the youngest and having everyone tell you what to do."

"It's not like she listens to anyone."

"Oh, Jam." Mama rubs my back. "You got your short fuse from me. I feel bad for you."

"What do you mean?"

"My mom was always on my case for my quick temper when I was growing up. I never understood why it mattered so much until I became a wife, and a mother, and I've had to work so hard to keep it in check."

"But you're hardly ever angry."

"I'm angry often, Jam. It's my first reaction when I'm stressed out or scared. I struggle to make sure it doesn't control me, or control what I say or do. Your father's helped me get a handle on my emotions over the years, but it hasn't been easy."

I think of the times I've seen Mama's lips pressed into a line, or seen emotion on her face that she didn't express. I've never recognized it as anger before.

"You're the same way, Jam," Mama continues. "Your default reaction in many situations—like when you're frustrated or embarrassed or hurt—is anger. But you need to rein it in. For your sake, and for others."

Mama may be right. Maybe I am quick to get angry sometimes. But it's never been a problem. Not for me, anyway.

"Can you try to work on it too?" Mama asks. "Take deep breaths when you feel your temper rising. Start now, while you're still young. It'll make life better for you. Believe me."

"I guess. But you do see what I'm saying about Aleeza, right?"

"She's missing your dad. Just like you are. It's an adjustment for everyone."

It's been a rough week, and we've all been grumpy. We've been FaceTiming Baba in the morning and at night, but somehow that makes him seem farther away. It's weird to see him sitting alone in an apartment that's furnished like a hotel room, with high ceilings and marble floors that make his voice echo. By the time each of us speaks to him for a few minutes, it's been half an hour. A couple of times Mama went into her room to talk privately. I want to do that too, instead of having my sisters impatiently crowd around me, listening in and interrupting.

"Can I talk to Baba by myself tonight?" I ask.

"What?"

"I want a normal conversation, without everyone telling me to hurry up, or trying to grab the iPad."

"Sure, but you know tonight means it's early in the morning for him. So you have to keep it short so he can get ready for work."

"I will." I suddenly feel lighter.

"Come on." Mama leans over and gives me a kiss on the cheek. "Get up and get ready, and let's have some breakfast."

"Okay."

"And remember what I said, please. It's good you look out for Bisma. But don't make Aleeza feel like you're against her. She's your sister too."

"Fine." I agree with my mom, so she won't be more stressed out than she already is. But I stand by what I said. Aleeza can be a total brat, and she better not get worse now that Baba isn't here.

14

Travis is standing at the whiteboard, writing down notes as the rest of the members of the newspaper club yell them out. We're brainstorming for the first issue of the paper, and, like always, I'm prepared with a long list of ideas. I'm staring at Travis, who's returned to school this year with longer hair and stubble on his upper lip. It gives him a bit of a skater vibe, but I'm more curious to see how he acts as editor in chief.

"How about something about the library?" Callie suggests.

"What about it?" Travis says.

"Maybe trends Ms. Hirschhorn noticed. Like which grades use it the most and stuff like that."

Travis scribbles "library story" on the board.

"How about interviewing her about how many books are overdue or missing, and if we should start a fine system like the public library?" Callie adds.

"I like that." Travis taps the lid of his marker against his teeth. "Maybe it could be an editorial debate with the pros and cons of starting that up."

He adds "fines" underneath "library." I stifle a groan. Seriously? Could this newspaper be any more boring?

"What else?" Travis pushes.

"What about an article about where the money from the fund-raisers we have goes?" I offer.

"What are you talking about?" Travis asks.

"I heard that a lot of the money kids raise selling wrapping paper and chocolates and stuff goes to the company that makes them, and only a tiny bit goes to our school. We can investigate," I explain.

Travis seems reluctant. "I don't know," he says.

"Why not? We can expose the truth," I argue.

"But it's not something you can change if that's just the way it works."

"We can change how we fund-raise!" I argue. Travis may look different, but his attitude is the same. He seems much more interested in everyone else's ideas than mine. And the fluffier the stories, the more he seems to like them.

Travis prints "fund-raisers" in letters that appear smaller than the rest of the ideas written on the board.

"How about a story about the exchange student from England?" Thu calls out.

"Who?" Travis asks.

"He's in my math class. His name is Ali."

"He's not an exchange student," I correct. "He moved here."

Travis adds "Ali" to the board. Seeing his name written there makes my palms sweat like when I'm in trouble. I wonder if it's because it feels like *he* is, or if it's because he's a topic for discussion along with the cafeteria rules and bell schedule.

My mind isn't fully here today, ever since fighting with Aleeza this morning. We ignored each other during breakfast, and she sulked over her soggy frosted flakes in a different shirt—one of her own. I considered it a victory as I ignored pleading looks from Mama that I know meant "be kind." I'm as kind as Aleeza deserves.

The group continues for another few minutes, until there's a list of about fifteen possible article ideas.

"Let's vote," Travis says. I halfheartedly raise my hand for the topics I hate the least and am startled when I hear my name.

"Jameela, can you take the Ali story, since you know him?" Travis asks.

"Uh, yeah. I guess so."

"Do you think he'll want to be featured?"

"I don't know." Ali hasn't shared much with me about his personal life, and I honestly don't know how he might react to the idea. "What do you want the article to be about?"

"Maybe the difference between school here and in England?" Thu suggests.

"Or another interesting angle," Travis adds, which isn't helpful. Maybe he's trying to pretend that he's supportive of me, despite the fact that he didn't vote for my suggestions. My fund-raiser idea wasn't chosen. And although several people voted for an editorial on how I think we deserve a student lounge like the teacher lounge, Travis put it on the "maybe" pile for next issue. I forgot to suggest the football-ban article. Maybe next time.

When the bell rings, I'm still thinking about how I'm going to get through this year with Travis. I can't let him stand in the way of writing the stories I want to write—that I *need* to write. I'm so deep in thought that I don't watch where I'm going.

THWACK!

"Watch out!" An eighth grader with round glasses scowls at me as I slam into him.

"Sorry," I mumble.

"You all right?" I hear an unmistakable British accent behind me. It's Ali, watching me act flustered with teasing eyes.

"Yeah. Um, we were just talking about you."

"Who was?" Ali's eyes quickly turn serious.

"The newspaper club."

"Why? Am I already registered as an enemy of the printed word?" Ali smirks.

"Not yet. They want to do a feature on you."

Ali stops walking.

"Was it your idea?"

"No!" I say quickly. "Some girl named Thu. She thought you were an exchange student."

"Oh."

"They asked me to write it, since I said I know you."

"Really."

"Is that cool? Are you in?"

Ali pauses to consider it.

"Can I trust you to make me sound good?"

"Yeah. Maybe you can come by after school some day, and we can work on it?" I feel heat rise to my face as I picture myself standing in the hallway, talking to a curly-haired Brit with dark eyes who everyone thinks is cute.

"Sure. See you later."

Ali walks away, and I wonder what kind of material he will give me for the story. I hope he opens up to me, because whatever angle I take for this story, I need it to be the best one I've ever written.

15

Can I have an application please?" Lily asks a man in a sea-green Yogurtland T-shirt.

"Hold on," the man grunts, disappearing under the counter. He reappears with a bent business card.

"Here. Apply online."

"Great, thanks," Lily says sweetly, but the man grunts again.

"You sure you want to work here? With that guy?" I whisper as we walk away.

"I'll work anywhere that'll hire me. This is better than the movie theater."

"I'd pick the movie theater." I gaze at sixteen flavors of frozen yogurt lining the wall and a bar filled with every topping you can dream of, and for a second think this might be the perfect place to work. Then I watch a frazzled mom yell at her son for spilling a blob of the yogurt on the floor. A moment later an elderly man complains that the peaches-and-cream yogurt is too runny and demands a new cup. Yeah, I'd pick the movie theater.

"The smell of the fake popcorn butter every day would make me sick." Lily smooths her long hair into a ponytail. "Plus I could live on yogurt."

"Did you get your work permit yet?"

"After my birthday. You have to be fourteen."

"Why are you in such a hurry to work?"

"I need to make money."

"What for?"

"I'm saving for this writing camp in Savannah next summer. It's expensive, though."

"So your mom's okay with you having a job?"

"Totally. She thinks it's good for me to 'learn the value of money.'"

There's no way my parents would let me work yet, no matter what it was for. When Maryam asked if she could get a job last year, since she was old enough get a work permit, it took a long time for them to finally agree.

"You have the rest of your life to work. Focus on

school, and we'll worry about the rest" is what Baba argued. But Maryam finally convinced him and Mama to let her babysit for some kids in the spring, since the family lived in our neighborhood and paid well, and the job was playing with two cute little kids after school twice a week. Maryam told me that she didn't want to have to ask for things like clothes she wanted or makeup when she knew our family didn't have money to spare. And recently, there was less when Baba wasn't working. I wonder if I should have offered to get a job too. But I have nine months to go until my fourteenth birthday, and I probably would have gotten the same answer.

"I'm entering the contest again," Lily says.

I was thrilled when Lily won the county's Combating Hate Through the Arts writing contest last year after she wrote a story about a kid who bullies a Muslim girl for wearing a headscarf but then realizes he's wrong. It was extra meaningful because she said my family had inspired her story, although none of my sisters or I have ever been harassed like that, and none of us wear the hijab. We've heard plenty of stories about people being mistreated, and Lily and her family are into standing up for anyone facing injustice. I made sure we included an announcement of her award in the *Crossing*, with a photo of her holding her certificate.

"What are you going to write about this year?" It'll be difficult for her to top last year's story, which included alternating perspectives and had an unexpected twist at the end.

"I started a story based on kids who have autism. Something about how music brings different people together and helps them understand each other."

"I'm sure it'll be awesome." Lily entering and winning the contest was what made me see for the first time that kids can win awards too. And it showed me that our words can make as much of a difference as adults' do—if we can get an audience that's bigger than our teachers and parents. I started to search for journalism contests and awards for middle schoolers, like the one I'm going to enter, and to take the school newspaper extra seriously.

"I doubt I'll win two years in a row, but I want to enter anyway. Maybe I'll place."

"I'm writing an article about Ali for the paper," I volunteer while I fill a small cup halfway with mango yogurt and top it with a few coconut flakes and Fruity Pebbles. They charge by the ounce at Yogurtland, so I'm careful to make sure it won't cost more than the five dollars I have in my pocket.

"Wait. For real?" Lily gives me a sideways glance and

dumps crushed Oreos over her Nutella yogurt. This girl can't get enough chocolate.

"We're doing a feature on him, the new foreign student."

Lily grins.

"It wasn't my idea!"

"Sure it wasn't." Lily squeezes my arm while we find a place to sit.

"I'm serious. Travis asked me to write it because I'm the only one on staff who knows him. I have no idea what to focus on." I taste my yogurt. It's sweet and tart and cold against my teeth.

"Sounds like an excuse to spend more time together."

"No, really. It's not," I snort. "Besides, he's into Maryam."

"He said so?" Lily's eyes grow wider, and she puts her spoon down to fully focus on me now.

"No."

"So you mean he checks her out?"

"Kind of."

"That doesn't mean anything. Everyone checks her out. She's drop-dead."

"I know." I sigh.

"Does she like him?" Lily asks.

"No!" I answer quickly. "I mean, I don't think so. It doesn't seem like it."

"I see you guys talking in the halls. Are you close?"

"He says hi and stuff. He always runs into me."

"Yeah, I'm sure it's a coincidence." Lily rolls her eyes.

"It is," I insist. "And besides, it's not like I'd go out with him or anything anyway."

"Why not?" Lily asks.

"My parents would freak out. We're not allowed to date."

"Then how are you supposed to meet someone?"

"I don't know. We haven't talked about that. But I don't think any of the Muslim kids I know are allowed."

It's true that we haven't discussed boys much in my family. I get the sense it's a subject my parents don't want to get into with us yet. But I know enough from the conversations we have had to understand that my parents don't expect me to date in a typical way, just like they didn't. Mama was finishing college in Florida, where she was born and raised, when she was introduced to Baba, a graduate student in Atlanta. Some mutual friends had a dinner party, and afterward they talked on the phone. They got engaged pretty quickly, once their families met and they knew they wanted to get married.

"My parents said I can start dating when I'm sixteen," Lily says. "But I don't know if I'll want to. At least not anyone we're in school with now."

"Yeah." I can't see Lily with any of the boys we know. She seems more mature than most of them. "Anyway, I hope Ali gives me something interesting to write about."

"You can always tie something he says to something else happening at school or in the world. Can't you?"

"I guess so."

"Well, whatever it is, I'm sure it will be a better story than how it saves the school money if you cover your textbooks."

"That was a Travis classic," I say, scraping the last of the yogurt out of my cup. I love Lily. She gets my frustration over what the newspaper could be, but isn't.

"I don't know how it's going to go with Ali," I add. "Sometimes he's friendly and talkative, and then he gets quiet and distant. And I want to write something good enough to enter into the National Media Contest."

"I'm sure you'll get a great story," Lily assures me, and I want to believe her. "And who knows what else will happen."

She smiles into her cup, and I know what she's

thinking. But it's not like I'm about to start liking someone just because my friends think he's cute or because he's funny and has a British accent. That isn't going to happen. And even if it could, I'm pretty sure he has a thing for my sister.

16

I'm going to be late tonight. Please get dinner ready. Bake the covered dish at 400 for 25 minutes. Make a salad. Set the table. Thanks, Mama.

My mother texts in full sentences and signs them like letters. She's at work for an evening shift today. I write k back. And a few seconds later Maryam's text comes through.

Sure. Love you, she says.

When Lily's mom drops me home from the yogurt place, Maryam is in her usual spot at the dining room table with her headphones on and a book flipped open. Aleeza is lying on the family room floor watching cartoons. But Bisma isn't with her.

"Where's Bisma?" I ask.

"I don't know," Aleeza mumbles. Maryam doesn't hear me.

I head up to our room, and Bisma emerges from the bathroom, bleary eyed.

"What's the matter?" I scan her tear-streaked face, and rage bubbles up inside me. "Did Aleeza do something else?"

"She didn't do anything." Bisma shakes her head.

"What is it then?"

"My neck hurts. See this bump?" She juts out her chin.

"I can't see anything. Where?"

"Right here." Bisma runs her fingers along the top of her neck.

I reach out my hand toward her, and Bisma jumps back.

"Don't touch! It's been like this for a few days, but it's hurting more now." Bisma's eyes fill up. "What's wrong with me?"

"Nothing's wrong with you." I try to soothe her.

"How you do know?"

"I just do. Remember when you thought you had tuberculosis?"

"I was coughing a lot."

"Everyone gets coughs. And then remember you were convinced you had Lyme disease?"

"I had a fever for three days."

"Yeah, but you weren't bitten by a tick. You need to stop reading Baba's health journals."

"But there are so many terrible diseases," Bisma sniffs.

"You'll worry yourself sick if you think you have all of them."

"What about my neck?" Bisma gingerly touches it again.

"Nothing's wrong with you," I repeat. "You probably slept funny. I get cricks in my neck once in a while."

"You do?"

"Yeah. It's probably a pulled muscle. Inshallah, it'll be fine soon. Want to put some ice on it?"

Bisma nods and sits down on her bed, and I go back downstairs to get it for her. I walk past Maryam, absorbed in her books, and almost stop to tell her that she had no idea her little sister was crying upstairs alone. But I don't. Bisma has always turned to me first, after our parents.

I grab a reusable ice pack from the freezer, wrap a dishtowel around it, and go back upstairs. Bisma takes it with a grateful smile and lies on her bed, resting the ice on her neck.

"I miss Baba," she says in a quiet voice.

"Me too." I wonder if she's wishing he were here to reassure her that she's fine, like he always does. I know I do. But I don't want her to start to cry again. So I change the subject.

"I'm writing an article about Ali for the school newspaper."

"Really?" As expected, Bisma's face brightens at the mention of Ali's name. "About what?"

"I'm not sure yet. I have to decide."

"Can I help?"

"Sure." I say that now, but I know it will be hard for her to help me. If anything, she'll get in the way. Ali is sweet to her and Aleeza whenever he sees them. I feel bad for him when he visits and the two of them smother him and battle for his attention. But he's nice enough to play a game with them each time.

"When's it due?"

"I'm the features editor. So as long as I get it in before we print, it's fine."

"Where's Mama? Shouldn't she be home?"

"Soon. She's working late tonight. Oh, wait. We're supposed to warm dinner." I remember her instructions.

"Maryam!" I yell.

No answer. The headphones are probably on.

"Aleeza!" I yell again.

"What?"

"Can you turn the oven on to four hundred?"

"What?"

"Turn the oven on to bake at four hundred."

"How?"

"Ugh. Forget it." I peel myself off the bed and go back downstairs to do it myself. Between the fighting this morning and dealing with Bisma's tears now, I'm ready to eat dinner, take a long shower, and finally talk to my dad in peace.

17

"Hey, Jam!" Baba's smile is so wide it almost fills the screen on Mama's tablet. "How are you?"

"Good." I stare at my father's face, and a pang of missing him strikes at my heart.

"Why are you alone? Where is everyone?"

"Mama said I could talk to you by myself."

"Why?" Baba's forehead wrinkles.

"I wanted to speak to you without everyone interrupting me for once."

"Oh. That's a good idea. So what's going on?" Now I can only see Baba's forehead, the ceiling of his apartment, and some modern metal light fixtures.

"Can you tilt the phone down? I can't see you anymore."

Baba's whole face is back on the screen.

"That's better."

"What's going on? How's school? How's newspaper, Miss Features Editor?"

I fill Baba in and tell him about the article I've been assigned to write.

"That could be fun," he says.

"Maybe. I don't want it to be another fluff piece. I want to write about the real things in Ali's life—like the serious stuff."

"Then you should."

"I get the feeling he doesn't want to talk about those things."

Baba pauses.

"You know that your grandfather interviewed many famous people, right?"

"Right."

"No matter who he was talking to, whether it was the new prime minister of Pakistan or leaders of other countries, popular actors, or members of the national cricket team, he had the same strategy. He would say, 'I let them talk, and they lead me to the story.'"

"What about asking probing questions? Didn't he do that?"

"Well of course there's that part too. But he used to

say that you can't go into a story with your own agenda. Respect people enough to tell you the story they want to tell after they are comfortable with you, and it'll turn out better that way. Get it?"

"I think so. Is that what you did when you wrote for your paper in college?"

"Well, I tried." Baba shrugs. "But I didn't produce anything that was going to win me prizes like Dada."

I remember Baba telling me that his mom was afraid he would become a journalist like his father, and how she discouraged him from writing and pushed him toward science. I think that's why he makes a point of telling my sisters and me to do what we love. And he's made sure to encourage whatever we're interested in, whether it's art for Aleeza, music for Bisma, or writing for me. Baba was Maryam's biggest fan before she stopped playing sports. He's not big on her fashion obsession, since Baba wears his clothes until they fall apart or Mama threatens to burn them. I guess it's another thing we have in common.

My eyes fall on the grainy black-and-white photo of my grandfather on my parents' dresser. Unlike the ones in the family room, where he's accepting awards or doing business, this image is of him and my grandmother a few years before they passed away. Neither of them is smiling, but they aren't smiling in any of the photos I've seen of them. I think people were a lot more serious in the olden days.

"I'm going to make a real difference, like Dada did. Starting with this year," I say. "And win prizes, too." I don't add that it's especially for Baba, and something to make him really proud.

"I don't doubt it. Make sure you e-mail me your story."

E-mail. Suddenly Baba seems thousands of miles away again.

"I miss you, Baba."

"I miss you too. Is everything else good?"

"Yeah. Except Aleeza's annoying."

Baba shakes his head at me. "Yeah, yeah. So nothing new, I guess."

"How's your work?"

"Busy. There's so much to do, and we need to hire more staff quickly. But I'm having trouble finding qualified people."

"Are you still coming back home when you're supposed to?"

"That's the plan, inshallah."

"Do you like it there?"

"I'm slowly figuring out how things work around

here. It's a different culture. But I was invited to a meeting at a hotel called the Emirates Palace yesterday. It's so fancy there's a vending machine for gold in the lobby."

"Seriously?" That sounds like a joke, or something you'd see in a cartoon.

"I can't make this stuff up. Instead of candy bars, you can buy bars of solid gold. You should see this place. It's so over the top. I'll send you guys pictures of it and the Sheikh Zayed Mosque. I got to pray there on jummah. It's very beautiful."

I'd like to see the vending machine in real life, and the mosque, too. Baba tells us little things about life in Abu Dhabi when we talk, and so far I know a lot of people from different countries work there, many very rich people live there, and it's hotter than Atlanta, which is hard to imagine. It's cool that Baba gets to go to nice mosques for Friday prayers. He also said there are special rooms to pray in inside malls and parking garages. That, along with hearing the call to prayer five times a day, makes it easier to be regular with prayers.

"I have to get ready for work soon. It's almost six thirty a.m. here. Can you get your sisters and Mama so I can say hi real quick?"

"Yeah."

"This was nice, though. I liked talking to you alone. You watching the game this weekend?"

"Maybe. It's not the same without you."

"I know. I wish I was watching with you."

"Me too."

"Love you, Jam. Shaba khair." Baba says what he always says to me at bedtime, even though he's just starting his day.

"Love you, Baba."

I stick my head out the door of the bedroom, expecting to yell, but Maryam and Aleeza are standing there, waiting to talk to Baba. I hear Bisma playing on her keyboard downstairs, practicing the song she was working on with Miss Jasmin last week.

"He wants to talk to you," I say, happy that I had my time but feeling guilty knowing that they each will only get a quick hello now. I'm in a better mood than I've been in all day, and I get ready for bed feeling excited about my interview with Ali, which we scheduled for next week. I'll try to take my grandfather's advice and let Ali lead me to the story.

18

Mama's lips are pressed together so tight I can barely see them.

"I didn't say yes," Maryam repeats.

"Why'd he think he could ask you?"

"I don't know. I've never talked to Seth before. We have math together." Maryam twists her long hair into a knot on top of her head.

"So he surprised you with this, out of the blue, during math class?" Mama looks unconvinced.

"Not during class. He came up to me afterward."

"And he presented you, someone he's never spoken to before, with . . . this elaborate gift? It makes no sense. When I was in high school, no one did anything like this." Mama points to the white box lying on the coffee table.

I peer into the box again. There are six jumbo chocolate-covered strawberries inside. But these aren't regular chocolate-covered strawberries. The dark chocolate is decorated with white chocolate lines to look like each berry is wearing a tuxedo. They're adorable. Seth wrote *I'd be BERRY happy if you went to Homecoming with me* on the lid of the box. Aleeza and Bisma cooed over how cute they thought that was. I think it's pretty cute too, even if it's cheesy.

"He was like, 'Can I talk to you for a minute?' and I said yeah, and then he opened up the box and stood there." Maryam changes her voice when she does Seth's part, and I can picture a sweaty, nervous kid fumbling with the box.

"What did you say?" Aleeza asks.

"I think I said something like 'oh wow.' I was totally caught off guard."

"But you took the berries?" Mama says.

"What was I supposed to do? Leave them in his hand? That would be so rude, right?" Maryam asks. Aleeza and Bisma nod enthusiastically in agreement. I hesitate.

"Yeah," I finally agree. It might have been rude.

"I understand you didn't want to be rude. But now he thinks you're going with him?" Mama asks.

"I didn't say yes!" Maryam's eyes grow bigger. "And

I don't want to go with him. This is what people do for homecoming now. They do something big when they ask people to go. Girls ask guys, too."

"I think you should give them back," Mama says.

"Nooo!" Aleeza pets one of the berries with her finger. "They're so cute."

"Don't touch them!" Mama scolds.

"We should eat them," I say. "The chocolate is already starting to slide off the strawberries. The box will be a mess by tomorrow."

"But you can't keep them." Mama falters. "It wouldn't be right. They must have been expensive."

"It would be so embarrassing if I took them back to school tomorrow. For him. It's not like he can give them to someone else now. Everyone already saw him give them to me."

"Can I have one? Please?" Aleeza is eyeing the one she touched.

"Fine." Mama sighs. "You probably left a fingerprint on it anyway."

"Yes!" Aleeza lifts the berry out of the box and nibbles on the tip.

"This has to happen when your father isn't here," Mama adds, as if she's thinking aloud. "I don't know what you're supposed to do."

"I think it's a good thing he isn't here for this," Maryam mutters under her breath, and our eyes meet for a moment. My parents may not have said too much to us directly about boys yet, but when we were at a wedding last year, a couple of aunties who are known for introducing people for marriage purposes started to ask Mama questions about Maryam, and Baba flipped out.

"Tell those sharks to stay away from my girls!" I remember him fuming at home later that night. "Don't they know she's a child? I told you not to let her wear heels. She can pass for twenty when she's done up."

The next day he showed us a new gray hair and said he was going to name it Maryam.

"What are you going to say to him?" Bisma finally asks what we're all thinking.

"Baba?" Maryam asks.

"No, Seth."

"Maybe 'Thank you, but I'm not allowed to go'?" Maryam asks Mama, who nods.

"Yes. Say that you have a very strict mother who forbids you." Hearing Mama refer to herself like that in the third person makes Bisma and me giggle.

"Maybe you can give him a different gift back," Bisma suggests.

"Yeah, like a big raspberry," I say.

"Where do you find a big raspberry?" Mama asks.

"Right here." I stick out my tongue and blow, making a wet fart sound. Everyone starts to laugh, including Mama.

"Poor Seth," Bisma says, shaking her head when Aleeza offers her a strawberry. "It was nice of him to ask you."

"Yeah, it was." Maryam starts to blush, and I'm suddenly impressed by Seth, cheesy pun or not. It took guts to go up to the prettiest girl in the grade, or maybe the entire school, and ask her to the dance. I'm feeling sympathy for this kid, when the doorbell rings and startles us.

"Who's that?" Aleeza asks.

"It's Ali, coming over for our interview." I realize he was supposed to be here an hour ago, and he's late.

19

So do you know the guy?" Ali asks me. We're sitting at the dining table, in Maryam's usual spot, and I've got Mama's laptop open in front of me.

"Who?"

"Mr. Strawberry." He points to the tuxedo-dressed strawberry on a dessert plate next to him. Aleeza made sure to present one to him and fill him in on the afternoon's events as soon as he walked in the house. It took my best threats to get her to go away so we could work in peace without her chattering or interrupting constantly. Bisma was complaining about her neck hurting again, so she and Mama went upstairs to rest. She's been taking medicine after going to the doctor, who thinks she has an infection. Maryam is on the phone in the kitchen with her best friend Saira, and I can hear snippets of them dissecting every moment of her encounter with Seth as she does the dishes.

"I have no idea who he is," I tell Ali.

"So that's a thing here? You give people fruit when you invite them to dances?"

"Guess so."

"Does she fancy the bloke?" Ali cuts into the strawberry with his fork. More like stabs it, actually. I smile at his word choice. Ali sounds extra British sometimes.

"No," I say. "She doesn't even know him."

"Oh." Ali examines the strawberry, shoves the whole thing into his mouth at once, and chews in silence.

"Should we start the interview now?" I ask.

"Sure."

As I open up the file with my questions, Ali speaks again.

"Is she going to go with him?" He sounds casual, but he's looking at me so intently that I realize he's jealous. Of Mr. Strawberry!

"No."

"Why not?"

"We're not allowed to go to dances with boys." I don't add that Maryam was just telling her friend on the phone that she honestly wouldn't want to go with

Seth. She was relieved to have an excuse to say no.

"What do you mean not allowed?"

"What do you mean what do I mean?"

"You're not allowed to go to a dance?"

"Not with a boy, like on a date." I pause. "Why? What's the big deal?"

"Do your parents think you're going to have an arranged marriage?"

"I don't know." My face grows warm. "That's kind of far away."

"Do they think none of you are going to go on dates?"

"I didn't say that!" I snap, my embarrassment turning to anger. "I'm only in middle school. And Maryam is in ninth grade! And—" I stop speaking. "I thought I was doing the interviewing."

"I'm just saying." Ali leans back in his seat, and his smirk settles in around his lips. "You don't seem like the type to sit around and wait for marriage proposals."

"I'm not waiting around for anyone for anything. And I have years before I need to think about that," I say as dismissively as I can, trying to hide how irritated I am.

"Okay," Ali says.

"Okay."

There's a long silence while I pretend to concentrate

on the computer screen. But I'm trying to calm myself down. Who does Ali think he is? He doesn't know anything about our family.

"So what about you? Are you going to be one of those kids who date in middle school?" The words come tumbling out of my mouth before I can get back to the interview.

"I don't know. Maybe."

"And then what?" I picture Ali at school, walking through the halls holding hands with a faceless girl, like a few of the other eighth graders do. Although if he likes Maryam, he's probably not interested in anyone at our school.

"Then nothing."

Uncle Saeed didn't allow his kids to date in high school. It was a big deal when his son Samir was caught with a secret girlfriend during his senior year. Most of the parents in our community seem to think that way, and I've never thought about how they expect their kids to eventually meet people.

"What about your parents?" As soon as the word "parents" slips out of my mouth, I bite my lip. It's a habit. But I should have said "mom." Or "mum."

"My parents met when they were in high school in East London and fell in love." I slowly exhale, relieved that Ali thinks I was asking him how his parents got together, although I meant what would they think about him having a girlfriend.

"That's sweet," I say.

"I guess. Except their parents didn't approve of their marriage, so it wasn't easy for them."

"Why not?"

"My grandmother wanted my father to marry someone else she had picked for him, and she was never nice to my mum. And then my mum's family resented my dad. It was complicated. But they were happy together. Until . . ." Ali focuses on something behind me as he says the last word, but it hangs in the air long after it leaves his lips.

"How about we leave marriage and family drama out of the article?" I try to change the subject, but I'm still thinking of Ali's mother, fighting for love, and then losing her husband so young.

"Good idea." Ali forces a little smile.

"Do you have opinions about life in America?" It's a broad question, but I think about what my dad said and hope it sparks an idea for a story.

"I always have opinions." Ali smiles for real.

I don't bother to type while Ali talks about how hot and sunny it is here compared to London. That's no surprise. He mentions how gigantic portions are at restaurants and how many napkins people grab and waste. I've never thought about that before, but I can see it. Then he says something about how people in America speak funny.

"Wait a minute," I interrupt. "You think *we* speak funny?"

"You do."

"Seriously? Have you ever had trouble understanding people?"

"All the time. I act like I can follow."

"Really? Even me?"

"Even you."

"Did something funny ever happen because you didn't understand somebody?"

"The other day this kid said he liked my pants. I thought he was talking about my underpants and was like, 'What?' But he was talking about my trousers."

That makes me giggle. "Trousers? Like dress pants?"

"No. Like trousers. We refer to what you wear under your trousers as pants."

We laugh at the mix-up, and I notice how different Ali is when he isn't serious or sad. There's a light that isn't there otherwise, and his eyes are bright.

Mama comes into the dining room and flicks on the

chandelier after we've been talking for at least an hour. Ali's in the middle of telling me about his old neighborhood and the man on the corner who sold fake designer purses on a cloth on the street.

"He'd see a police officer and pull the string, which would scoop up the purses into a bundle so he could run. But then he'd be back the next day."

"Don't you kids want to eat?" Mama asks. "It's time for dinner."

"Yes, please," Ali says.

"Sure," I agree, although I'd rather keep talking. I know Ali better now. And he finally seems to be letting down his guard a bit. But I'm nowhere closer to finding the story I want to tell.

20

Six big square pads are lined up in a row on the field, with round targets in the middle of them. We're standing in our groups during gym class for our unit on archery. I've got Lily and Kayla with me, along with three other girls we're not friends with. It's overcast today and threatening to rain any minute, but at least it's not blazing hot.

"Make sure you hold the bow straight," Mrs. Woodruff instructs. "And the rest of you, stand behind the lines in the grass."

"This is so boring," Lily complains. "I thought we were doing tennis for our next unit."

"I'm fine with it," Kayla says. "We don't have to run around and get sweaty."

"I like it," I add. Archery is one of my favorite things to do in gym. I love the weight of the bow in my hand and the tension in my arms as I pull back an arrow and let it fly. Plus it's a sport where you don't have to depend on anyone but yourself, and you know exactly how you score right away. I only wish I could shoot more than three arrows in a row and get into a rhythm, instead of having to wait for five girls to go before my next turn.

"I'm up." Lily lifts the bow and takes an arrow out of the cone and aligns it on the bow. "I'm so bad at this."

ZING!

The arrow flies through the air, neatly misses the target by at least three feet, and lands somewhere in the grass.

"Told you I'm bad at this!" Lily giggles.

"You didn't aim," I say. "You have to focus on the target."

"I did." Lily starts to howl with laughter, and Kayla joins in.

"Like this." I take the bow and demonstrate how to fix your eyes past the tip of the arrow to the point where you want it to land.

Lily tries again and this time hits the outer edge of the target. No points, but at least it's something.

"YES!" Lily cheers. "You're the best!"

"You're so good at this," one of the girls behind us says. I think her name is Kenzie.

"Thanks," I say.

"It's like you're a natural," she continues. "But that makes sense, 'cause you're Indian, right?"

"What?" I don't know if I heard her right.

"She's not *that* kind of Indian, Kenzie," another girl named Maureen corrects. "You're thinking of Native Americans. She's from India."

It keeps getting worse. I can't believe what I'm hearing, and look at Lily and Kayla in disbelief. Lily palms her face with her hand.

"I'm not Indian," I tell Kenzie and Maureen. "I'm American."

"I mean, but where are you from . . . like, originally?" Maureen asks.

"My father and grandparents came to America from Pakistan. It's a different country from India."

"Got it. Sorry." Kenzie shrugs dismissively. She doesn't say it, but it feels like she means "same thing."

Lily fires her third arrow and misses the target again. This time she doesn't laugh, though. She hands me the bow in silence.

As I step up to the line, my face is ablaze with fury at myself for not speaking up. I want to say that Christopher Columbus may have been traveling to "India" when he ended up in the Caribbean, but most people have figured out the difference by now. And I want to say that I'm not good at archery because I'm Native American or Indian or Pakistani or American. I'm good at archery because I keep my eye on the target and manage to stay in control. If only I could apply the same principles to the other parts of my life.

I pull back my first arrow, tense my muscles, and aim.

ZING!

It hits the target. The outermost ring, but at least I got points.

I pull back the second arrow and this time hit the black ring. Lily and Kayla cheer for me.

Just as I'm about to fire the third arrow, I hear Maureen and Kenzie whispering. Kenzie is saying, "It was an honest mistake, okay? She knew what I meant. You didn't have to make a big deal about it."

I'm listening to them and don't focus on my third arrow. It flies into the grass.

"Oh man," Lily says. "I thought for sure you were going to hit the bull's-eye this time."

When we get the signal, I quietly collect my arrows.

I may have missed the target, but I've just figured out what I'm going to focus my article on. And it's going be everything I want it to be—hard hitting, covering a topic important enough to enter into the journalism contest, and something that'll make Baba truly proud.

21

She said that?" Ali is incredulous.

"Yup." I speak in a lower voice when the man at the table next to us in the library scowls from behind his computer to let us know we're disturbing him.

"What did you say?" Ali continues.

"I told her I was American. Of course that wasn't good enough."

"Right," Ali snorts. "At least when Brits say insulting things they have the decency to be accurate."

"Really?"

"Actually, no. Everyone who's brown is a Paki."

"Do you ever get called that?"

Ali traces the edge of his binder with his finger. "Yeah. Sometimes as a joke with my mates. Sometimes not."

"That sounds awful."

"It happens. What can you do?"

I take a deep breath. "Well, there *is* something you can do."

"What?" Ali looks doubtful.

I pull out my notebook. After gym yesterday, I took notes furiously during the rest of the day at school. I stayed up late last night doing research and finalizing the draft. And now I only need a few more quotes from Ali to have the story I wanted to write. It came together perfectly, and I'm feeling great about it. Finally!

"This." I proudly hand Ali the pages of the story, which I printed out on our ancient printer at home. The title, or future headline, reads PARDON ME? WHAT DID YOU SAY? Ali chuckles when he sees it.

"We can make a difference if we talk about the annoying things that kids have to deal with constantly—things like what Kenzie said to me and what your coach said to you about your mom."

"What?" Ali's smile disappears.

"If you give me some more examples, talk about how it felt, and how you wish it wasn't like that, and if people can put themselves in your shoes, maybe they can—"

"No." Ali stops me and starts to scan the article.

I wasn't done explaining.

"But—" I start again.

"I don't want to do that." Ali shakes his head slowly and hands me back the pages.

"Are you serious?" I want to push the article back at Ali and make him read the whole thing, but he's folded his arms and doesn't look interested.

"Completely."

"But why? This is a chance to make a difference!"

Ali pushes his hair off his forehead, and when he looks at me, his eyes are unreadable, and his tone is colder.

"I'm not your victim, for whatever you're trying to prove."

"What are you talking about?"

"I get you're upset about what Kenzie said to you. Or that you want some big story to write. But I thought people were curious about me, that you were. And that you wanted to write something about *me*."

I hear him speaking, but I'm also reviewing the points I listed in the notebook before I wrote the article. They make so much sense. If he finishes reading it, I'm sure he'll change his mind.

"This stuff happens a lot, though," I argue. "People don't realize the small things they say that are based on stereotypes and how hurtful they can be. There's even a word for it: microaggressions."

I wait for Ali as he stares back at me, expecting him to agree. "Come on," I press. "This is important."

"I thought *I* was." Ali pauses, and then adds, "You know, when I saw your title, I thought it was going to be about me understanding your American accent."

I reread the title. "Pardon Me? What Did You Say?" would have been clever if the article was about that. But it isn't. It's about something bigger.

The words Baba said about letting the story come to me buzz in my ears, like the vibration from a bow, but I ignore them as I fire my last arrow.

"The story *is* about you, but more than you. Kenzie said that thing, and the idea popped in my head. I think it'll be a powerful article that can make a difference. I was sure you'd want to be a part of it."

"I'm sorry, but I don't." Ali stands up, and I know I missed the mark. "Listen, you can write your article any way you please. But I don't want to be in it. I told you what I did about my life in private."

"Where are you going? Are you seriously going to leave?" My voice is loud enough that I get several annoyed stares.

"I told the guys I would play some foot—I mean *soccer* with them after I was done with the interview. We're done, right?"

"I mean, we can be, I guess, but—"

"Good luck." Ali shakes his head as if he can't believe his disappointment in me, even though I'm the one who's stunned by his reaction. He grabs his backpack and files out of the library. I'm left alone to sit and stew, my eyes stinging with the shock of losing the subject of my story—and maybe even a friend.

22

Mama?" I push the bedroom door open since it's ajar and find my mom sitting in bed, reading.

"Can I go to Lily's house after school today?"

"Hold on," Mama says into the book, and I notice her tablet is sitting on top of it. She clears her throat and looks at me.

"Oh. Sorry. I didn't know you were on the phone."

"I was almost done." Mama motions me into the room.

I glance at the iPad and see Baba's face.

"Salaam, Baba." I wave at him.

"Salaam, Jam." Baba's face is drawn and tired. He's wearing a suit and probably got back from work recently since it's evening in Abu Dhabi.

"How are you?" I ask.

"I'm fine. Ready for school?"

"Almost. So can I go to her house?" I ask Mama.

"Today? Sorry, no. I'm picking Bisma up from school early for the doctor. I need you to be home so Aleeza isn't alone. Maryam's babysitting today."

"The doctor? Again? Didn't you take her yesterday?" I peer at my mother's face and notice telltale signs that she's been crying.

"Yes, but he ordered another test for her, so I need to take her for that."

"What kind of test?"

"Nothing you need to worry about. Go eat something. Your bus will be here soon."

"What's wrong with Bisma?" A prickle runs down my spine. "What did her doctor say?"

Mama took Bisma back to the doctor during school yesterday to follow up about her neck, since the bump and pain she's been complaining about never went away. In fact, it got worse, even after she took antibiotics for a week, so the doctor ordered a blood test as well. Neither of them said much about how the appointment went, and I never asked for details, either. We went to Mellow Mushroom for a fund-raising night for Bisma and Aleeza's school, and everything seemed normal. I didn't pay attention at the time, but now that I think about it, Mama didn't say much at dinner and hardly touched her pizza.

"Don't worry, Jam." I hear Baba's voice and remember that he's still on FaceTime. "Inshallah, Bisma will be fine."

"But what is the test for?" My voice comes out higher pitched than usual.

"To rule out anything serious," Baba says.

"Like what?"

"Nothing. Please don't say anything to your sister. You know she'll panic. Dr. Gordon was very reassuring, and she's handling things fine right now." Mama's right about Bisma. I know how she probably feels, as I start to imagine terrible things. What if something is seriously wrong with my sister?

"I won't say anything to her," I promise. "But can you just tell me?"

"Go to school." Baba speaks up again, and this time his voice is firm. "All we can do is pray that everything will be fine."

I turn to Mama, and she squeezes my shoulder. Her eyes are pleading. I reluctantly get up to leave, say bye to my father, and give Mama a quick kiss on the cheek, dread gnawing at my insides. Whatever I'm seeing in my parents' expressions means this is something concerning.

The cupboard where we keep cereal is stuffed with boxes of our favorites. I pull out the Cinnamon Toast Crunch and start to pour a bowl, and a few crushed pieces, crumbs, and sugar from the bottom of the box fall out. Normally, I'm glad that since the middle school bus comes last in the mornings, I can have the kitchen table to myself if I wait for the others to leave. But at moments like these I wish I got to the cereal first. I settle for some Honey Bunches of Oats and sit down with the bowl and Mama's laptop, which she left on the table.

Mama is upstairs, so I flip open the laptop, turn it on, and type "Reasons for painful bump on neck" into Google. A box pops up with a photo of a woman and a doctor pressing on her neck, and the text next to it says that "a variety of conditions and diseases" can cause neck pain. That's not helpful. Then I see an article called "Neck lump: picture, causes, associated symptoms and more" and click on it.

I gasp as I see photos of people with giant lumps growing out of their necks next to the text. Each image is scarier than the last, and I instinctively put a hand on my own neck.

"What in the world are you reading?" Mama comes

up behind me and startles me. As I jump, the milk from my spoon splatters onto the computer screen.

"Oops! Sorry!" I run to grab some paper towels and clean it off. Luckily, nothing gets into the keyboard.

"Jameela," Mama sighs, and shuts the laptop after I gladly close the window with the bulging necks. "We told you not to worry about this."

"I can't help it."

Mama sits down on the chair next to me and sighs again.

"I should have known the reporter in you would win."

I've heard this a million times before. My parents like to say it whenever I'm curious about something. Mama speaks again, and this time her eyes are glistening.

"I don't want to worry you, or have you do things like this, and that's why I didn't tell you."

"But knowing that there's something you're not telling me is even worse."

"I know." Mama clears her throat. "So . . . well . . . ah . . . Dr. Gordon is worried that Bisma might have a lymphoma."

"A what?"

"It's a disease that impacts your lymph nodes."

"Disease" is a word we hear regularly in our house,

especially with the type of work Baba does. But thankfully, it's never been in relation to us, except for the times Bisma freaks out about having one and we have to convince her she doesn't. And now she might have one? An actual disease? How can this be happening?

"How do you get it? How will Dr. Gordon know if she has it? And then what?" My mind starts to race with questions, and Mama's expression changes to one of regret.

"No one knows how you get it. This test is a scan that will help determine if that's what it is, or not. So for now, we need to wait and see and hope that it's not that."

"But what else? There has to be something we can do!"

"Pray, Jameela. And stay off the Internet."

I don't say anything.

"Please promise me. I don't want you looking at things and getting worked up, especially when we don't know anything yet."

"Okay," I finally say. "I promise."

23

Hello? You there?"

Travis is standing over my seat. I've been staring at the cover of my notebook and didn't notice him.

"What's up?" I ask.

"I'm checking in with everyone about their sections. We need to send to print soon, so everything has to be in by tomorrow. You good?"

"Yeah."

"You edit your submission from Callie yet?"

"Which one?" I don't remember anything about a submission from her.

"The library profile."

"That's in my section?"

"Yes. We talked about it. Remember?"

"I thought it was going to be in editorial. A debate about starting fines for overdue books." I remember wanting to groan but being proud of myself for holding it in.

"We decided in the end to feature Ms. Hirschhorn. You were there. Weren't you listening?"

"Yes, I was listening. And it was the other way around."

Travis chews on the back of his pen and doesn't say anything for a second. The stubble on his upper lip has grown in more since our last meeting. It's like a tiny mustache, but I glance away so he doesn't think I'm admiring it, because I'm not.

"I'm pretty sure it wasn't." Travis finally speaks.

"I was featuring Ali, remember? Why would we feature two people?"

"A teacher and a student. It works." I know Travis just thought of that, and he seems pleased with himself.

"Yeah, but that isn't what we decided. And if I'm the features editor, don't I get to choose what goes in my section?" As soon as I say the last few words, I regret them and can guess what Travis will say next.

"I'm the editor in chief. So I make the final decisions." There it is. Travis crushes the notion that I have any real say over my section, or that he's changed. His long hair and new laid-back look are nothing more than appearances. He's the same uptight, bossy person he was last year. Except this year he thinks he has the right to be, since he's the one in charge.

I can't deal with him right now.

"So let's do both profiles, okay?" Travis smiles at me, but there's no warmth behind it.

"You're the boss. Whatever you say."

I expect Travis to go on to check in with the next person, but instead he sits down on the desk next to mine and crosses his legs.

"And what about your story?"

"What about it?"

"How's it going?"

"It's going." I don't know where yet, now that Ali ditched me, but I figure it's going somewhere. Travis waits for me to say something else, and when I don't, he finally stands up to leave. I exhale slowly. I managed not to fight with him, but it took a lot of effort. Maybe Mama's right. I am angry right now, and it probably has something to do with being frustrated, scared, and stressed all at once.

"Are you into this, Jameela?" Travis turns back to me.

"What?"

"You have a different attitude about newspaper this year. Is it because you don't like that I'm editor? Because Ms. Levy said that you—"

"Are you kidding me?" I try to keep my voice down, but it's shrill. "You think *I* have an attitude?"

"Yeah. I do."

"Maybe it's because you shoot down all my ideas."

"We vote," Travis says dismissively. "It's not my fault."

"You never vote for my ideas. Everyone else can tell that you don't like them." I accuse Travis of the thing that's been bothering me since last year.

"I can have opinions too," Travis scoffs. "Maybe your suggestions aren't as brilliant as you think."

Brilliant. That word reminds me that Ali didn't think so either.

"Anyway, I need you to be in this and committed to the paper," Travis adds.

"I'M COMMITTED!" I'm yelling, and I don't care. "WHO SAID I WASN'T COMMITTED!"

"Jameela!" Ms. Levy sticks her head out of her office. "Get in here."

I glare at Travis and drag myself over to Ms. Levy. She points at the small chair in front of her desk, and I go inside and try to close her door. The trash can is in the way, so I kick it aside and then go sit on the chair. Ms. Levy sits behind her desk and folds her arms.

"What was that about? Do you not remember what I told you about you two fighting?"

Anger is twisting through me like a tornado, and I'm afraid to open my mouth again. I don't know what I might say. How dare Travis accuse me of not caring about the paper? It's the thing I care most about at school!

"Jameela." Ms. Levy examines my face. "What's going on with you? You've been distracted and not acting like yourself. Is there something you want to tell me?"

I shake my head.

"Is anything going on at school that is bothering you?"

Another head shake.

"Are you sure?"

This time I nod my head.

"Is everything fine at home?"

I want to say yes, but I can't bring myself to do it. So I shrug.

"What's the matter?" Ms. Levy's tone is softer now. "You can talk to me, hon."

I start to shake my head again, but then the words start pouring out.

"My dad has to work in Abu Dhabi and he's so far away and I only see him on FaceTime."

"I had no idea. I'm sure that—"

"And my sister might have lymphoma."

Ms. Levy's eyes widen as I say the last sentence, and she bites her lower lip.

"Oh, honey. I'm so sorry."

I nod my head again. If I try to say anything else, I'm going to start to cry.

"Hopefully, your sister will be okay," Ms. Levy continues. "Lymphomas are often treatable cancers."

Wait a minute. What?

"*Cancer?*" It comes out in a whisper. "What do you mean cancer?"

Ms. Levy's face puckers like she swallowed something bitter.

"Lymphomas are a form of cancer. You didn't know that?"

No. I didn't. But I do know cancer is one of the scariest words I've ever heard. No wonder my parents were being so secretive. Tears wet my cheeks while Ms. Levy comes out from around her desk and awkwardly pats my shoulder.

"I'll talk to Travis," Ms. Levy mumbles. She hands

me a tissue from the box on her desk. "And ask him to give you some space."

I try to say thank you, but it comes out a garbled mess. All I can think as I blow my nose is, *It can't be cancer. Please, God, don't let it be cancer.*

24

I turn my key in the front door and am hit with a blast of air-conditioning as I walk inside. The TV is blaring, which means Aleeza is safely home from the bus stop.

"Hey," I yell out.

"Hey," Aleeza answers as I come up the stairs. She's sitting in the middle of the carpet and has art supplies spread out around her. There's a bowl of chips next to her and a pile of crumbs from where she either sat on some or stepped on them. Wherever Aleeza goes, a mess follows.

"What are you doing?" I ask. "How was school?"

"Fine. Making a card for Bisma."

"What for?"

"Because she has to go to the doctor." Aleeza holds

up the page, and I recognize her drawing. It's always the same: Baba, Mama, Maryam, me, Bisma, and Aleeza standing in a line, organized by age and height, even though Bisma and Aleeza are almost the same size in real life. There are grass and flowers underneath our feet, and a yellow sun shining down on us. Today a big rainbow is splashed across the page, and when I pay attention, I notice that instead of the stick figures Aleeza used to draw, these people have a lot more detail and actual clothes.

"That's really good," I say.

"Thanks. I can make you one."

"Do you want something else to eat?"

"No."

"You have to clean this up when you're done."

"I will."

I'm starving, so I help myself to the bag of barbecue-flavored chips Aleeza left open on the counter, some leftover pasta salad from the refrigerator, a banana, and a tall glass of milk. While I eat, my eyes fall on the laptop again. I promised Mama I would stay off the Internet. But why didn't she say lymphoma is cancer? And what does that mean for Bisma? As I think about it, my heart starts to pound, and I'm afraid I might throw up. I need to focus on something else, so I flip open the computer and edit my article, taking out Ali's name and any reference to his life. Instead I put in a few hypothetical situations as examples of microaggressions, define the term, and discuss how they harm people. When I'm done, the article isn't nearly as strong or as interesting as the original. But at this point, I need to turn something in before we go to print. I'm writing, but I keep thinking about Bisma, and the word "cancer" is swirling in my brain, making it hard to concentrate.

Next, I read Callie's article about the library and make a few minor corrections. It's way more entertaining than I thought it would be, because Ms. Hirschhorn has funny things to say about kids and the books they check out and some of the weird things she has found in returned books, like a letter to Santa and an apology letter someone wrote to his parents. I save both of the articles in the Google drive where the content for the first issue is stored, and then send an e-mail to Travis to let him know my submissions are ready to go. Finally, I shut the computer and mindlessly watch TV with Aleeza, although I'm listening for the door instead.

When I finally hear the rattle of the key turning in the lock, I run down the stairs.

"Oh. It's you," I say when Maryam appears, wearing her backpack and with headphones around her neck.

"Nice to see you, too," she replies.

"Sorry, I thought you might be Mama."

"She'll be home in an hour. What's the matter?"

"Did you hear about Bisma?"

"Yeah, she went to the doctor. Why? Did something happen?" Maryam clutches my arm.

"I don't know. They aren't back yet."

"You scared me! I thought something bad happened."

"It did."

"What?" Maryam drops her bag on the floor.

"Mama told me what they're testing for," I share.

"I know."

"Wait. You knew and didn't tell me?"

"It was late last night, and Mama told me what the doctor was worried about."

"Did she tell you it's a kind of . . . cancer?" The last word comes out in a whisper, as if saying it too loud will make it real.

"I knew that already."

"Mama didn't tell me."

"She probably didn't want you to freak out, Jam. She has enough to worry about, right? Plus, Baba isn't here."

I hadn't thought about that. I am freaking out, but I don't know how to stop.

Maryam joins me in the kitchen, but instead of eating anything, she pulls canisters of flour and sugar from the pantry.

"What are you doing?"

"I thought I'd make cookies for Bisma."

"Can I help?" I could use the distraction.

"Sure. Can you get the chocolate chips?"

We work together quietly, each of us lost in our own thoughts. Maryam measures out the ingredients while I soften the butter in the microwave. When the dough is ready, we roll it into balls and drop them onto a pair of well-worn cookie sheets.

"Don't do that!" Maryam cautions as I pop a ball of dough into my mouth. "It's got raw eggs in it."

"I know." Baba has warned us plenty of times about safe food handling and the risk of eating uncooked eggs. "But cookie dough is the best."

Maryam presses the balls down to flatten them a little. Her cookies are always perfectly moist and gooey.

"I'm scared about Bisma," I confess to her.

Maryam stops sprinkling salt on the tops of the cookies and turns to face me.

"I am too," she says. "I couldn't stop thinking about her all day. I'm pretty sure I bombed my geometry test."

"You probably just think that. I'm sure you did fine."

"I don't know. School isn't as easy for me as it is for you," Maryam sighs.

"You do well."

"Yeah, but I have to work twice as hard."

I never thought about that before. People tend to assume everything comes easily to Maryam because she's so pretty. Maybe even me.

"Do you think Bisma has it?" I ask.

"I hope not." Maryam brushes the hair off her face with the back of her hand. "It's all so awful to think about."

I don't ask her to elaborate.

The cookies are in the oven when we hear the door open again. Maryam grabs my hand, and we go downstairs to find Mama and Bisma.

As soon as I see my mother's face, I yelp, "No!"

Mama nods her head, puts her arm around Bisma, and pulls her close. Maryam and I surround them in a big hug. We say nothing, our hearts too full for words.

Aleeza comes bounding down the stairs, waving the card she made.

"What's going on?" She stops when she sees us. "Why is everyone sad?"

I pull away as Bisma smiles at Aleeza with a strength I've never seen before.

"I'm not sad, Leeza. I'm sick, but I'm going to be okay. Is that for me?"

We watch Bisma admire her card and thank Aleeza, who glows from the praise. Then the oven timer starts to beep, and we head upstairs for warm cookies.

25

Uncle Saeed pushes up his glasses and clears his throat.

"Inshallah, inshallah . . . God willing . . . she will beat this," he says. He and Farah Auntie came over as soon as Mama called them with the news. Ali came too, wearing a somber expression and carrying plastic bags filled with the dinner they brought us from Kabab Hut. Now he's sitting in the dining room, teaching Aleeza and Bisma a card game and making them both shriek with laughter, a sound that is sharply at odds with the mood in the house.

Ali glances over at my chair from time to time. I'm sharing it with Maryam for a change, and we are squeezed in together. I feel his eyes on us, but when I look up, he glances away. I'm guessing Maryam has his attention, since it was totally awkward between us when he walked in and said hi. Somehow he's managed to completely avoid bumping into me at school since our argument about the article. I want to kick myself for noticing what he's doing and who he's looking at, when it isn't what's important right now. But I do notice.

I've heard what the doctor said three times already—first when Mama gave us kids a watered-down version, then when I eavesdropped while she talked to Baba on the phone, and now while she tells Uncle and Auntie. What I've learned is that the doctors saw a twelve-centimeter mass that they called a lymphoma in Bisma's chest in a scan. I asked, and they confirmed it's a type of cancer. She has to go to the hospital tomorrow, and the doctors will try to figure out exactly what kind it is and what stage it is, which means how bad it is. Then they will decide what her treatment needs to be.

"I can't believe this is happening," Mama says as Bisma slaps a card on the table with a triumphant laugh. "She's been perfectly healthy and only started complaining about her neck recently. She didn't have any of the symptoms people with lymphomas sometimes get. That's why the doctor thought her elevated white count was due to an infection."

I grimace, remembering how I dismissed Bisma's fears when she first showed me the bump on her neck. I was certain that it was nothing, like usual. But she knew something was wrong, and she was right. Farah Auntie glances at me and gives me a sympathetic look as if she can hear my thoughts, and then rubs Mama's arm.

"No one could have known. We're here for you. Whatever you need. What can we do?" she says.

"Pray for her." Mama's voice cracks, and I have to look away as my throat starts to burn. Maryam grabs my hand, and I let her hold it instead of pulling it away like I want to. It's making the tears threaten to fall more.

"Is Faisal coming?" Uncle Saeed asks about Baba.

"He was very emotional when I told him. I had to stop him from getting on a plane tonight. He's going to talk to his supervisor and figure out what kind of leave he can take. Plus we need to make sure it doesn't impact our insurance."

"Do you have good coverage for . . . something like this?" Farah Auntie asks.

"I don't know." Mama sighs. "I guess so. We have to check."

"I'll help him figure it out," Uncle Saeed offers.

"Baba has to be here," I hear myself say. I thought I was only thinking it, so my voice startles me.

"I know, Jam, but it's complicated. He'll come as quickly as he can," Mama says. "Trust me—I want him here more than anyone."

I have so many questions. Like, if Baba leaves, will he lose his job? Will he have to start all over looking for something new? What if our insurance isn't good? Will Bisma be able to go to the doctors? How will we have enough money to pay for whatever she needs?

"Why don't you kids warm up the food so we can eat," Farah Auntie suggests. "You must be hungry, and it's getting late for a school night."

I know she's trying to send us away, but I jump up, relieved to leave the conversation anyway. Listening and thinking are making my head hurt. Maryam gets up behind me.

"Ali, can you help the girls, please," Farah Auntie calls out.

"We've got it." I don't want to interrupt the card game. But Mama tells Aleeza and Bisma to shower and change while dinner is warming, so Ali follows us into the kitchen.

"Are you guys all right?" he asks us. The coldness in his voice from the last time we spoke is gone, and his face is filled with concern.

"I want to understand what's going on." I stare at a crack in a tile on the floor.

"She's going to be okay," he says.

I nod and focus on unwrapping the naan from the white paper bag it's in, happy to have something to do with my hands. The bag is moist and soggy from the heat of the freshly baked bread. Ali opens up a container of beef kabobs.

"Do you have a plate to put these on?" he asks.

Maryam hands him a plate, and while he loads it up with the meat, he starts to speak.

"When my dad had his heart attack, I wasn't home. I went out after football training. I didn't tell my parents I was going to be late, and my phone was dead."

Ali finishes arranging the kabobs on the plate and then takes another container out of the bag, this one filled with orange pieces of barbecue chicken tikka. I quietly hand him another plate, afraid that he'll stop talking. I'm not sure if he's addressing Maryam or me, or both of us, but this is the first time he's shared anything about his father.

"When I got home, no one was there. And when I finally started charging my phone, I saw missed calls from my mum. So I called her back, and she was crying and yelled, 'Where were you? I was calling.' And I was angry, thinking she was overreacting to my being late. But then she said, 'We're at the hospital. Abba had a heart attack.'"

I gulp.

"Do you have a bowl for the chutney?" he asks. "Should we warm the kabob in the oven?"

I turn the oven on, and Ali continues to speak.

"My parents had eaten dinner without me, and afterward, my abba thought he was having indigestion. He complained about it for a bit, and then he collapsed. My poor mum was alone, trying to revive him while I was out with my mates at a chicken shop."

"I'm so sorry," Maryam says.

"By the time I got to the hospital, he was unconscious and hooked up to machines. They lowered his body temperature to try to let his body recover, and we waited for forty-eight hours to see if he would wake up."

"Did he?" I whisper.

"No." Ali's tone is bitter. "I never got to say goodbye to him. And the last thing he probably thought about me was wondering where the bloody hell I was."

"No," I say. "That can't be it."

"What?"

"I'm sure he thought about how much he loved you."

Ali shakes his head.

"We didn't get on the last couple years before he died. It was definitely my fault."

I'm so sad for him, but don't know what I could

possibly say to make a difference. Instead, I pull out a salad bowl and dump the lettuce and onions that are in a paper box into it. Ali's pain is so raw it stings like the onions hitting my eyes.

"Bisma is going to be okay," Ali repeats, pounding his fist on the counter. "She has to be."

I nod my head, and Maryam murmurs something I don't catch.

"Is it ready, kids?" Farah Auntie pops her head in the kitchen. "Should I call everyone?"

"Yes," I say, wiping my eyes. "We're ready."

Ali glances at me and squares his shoulders, as if he's putting the weight of his sorrow back on, for him to carry alone. The moment we shared is gone, yet the weight of his confession is piled on top of the fear that has engulfed my heart. Any negative feelings I had toward him about the article float away like the steam coming from the hot food. It doesn't matter anymore. He has to be right. Bisma has to be okay.

26

A hand taps my shoulder.

"What?"

"Jam . . . ?" It's Bisma whispering into my ear. "Are you awake?"

"No. What time is it?" I'm fully awake now.

"It's night."

"What's the matter? Are you feeling sick?" I struggle to sit up, worried.

"I'm fine. I—I want . . ." Bisma stops herself.

"What is it?"

"Can I sleep with you?"

"Did you have a bad dream?"

"Yeah."

My bed is a twin size, and I'm sprawled across it. But

I scoot over toward the wall, and Bisma slides in. She smells like the kids' coconut hair-and-body wash with monkeys on the bottle that's in the shower.

"It's just a dream." I echo what my parents used to say to me when I would go to their room, running my hand along the wall to steer myself through the dark hallway at night. "Think about nice things."

Bisma tucks her arm through mine and quickly falls asleep, but I'm awake now and watch her. I can make out her features from the streetlight shining outside our window. She looks the same as always, and it's hard to imagine that there's something as sinister as cancer running through her body.

When I hear the sounds of Mama getting up for Fajr prayers, I squint to see the numbers on the clock across the room and read 4:33 a.m. For a moment I consider getting up to join her, but Bisma is breathing lightly and might wake if I move, so instead I pray as hard as I can from my bed.

"Please, God, make my sister get better quickly. Mama says that you only give people burdens that they can bear. But I don't think I can bear anything bad happening to Bisma. Please make it easy for her, and make the stage of her . . . cancer . . . not so bad. Please make her treatment be quick and not hurt. And please let Baba be able to be with us soon. Ameen."

As I mention Baba, I remember how he always starts his duas with praise and thanks for God, and that he asks for blessings for his messengers and for everyone around the world, not just our family. I only asked for a bunch of stuff, so I decide to add more.

"And also, Allah, you are the most gracious and most merciful. Thank you for everything you've given us. For our food, and our house, and our family and everything. Please help all the people in the world who are suffering. Please make it easier for Ali and his family to deal with his dad dying and be at peace, and bring them together soon. I know I'm asking for a lot of things, but Baba says you want us to turn to you as much as we need to, and to ask for the things we want. So I hope you don't mind that it's a lot. Ameen."

I feel better, close my eyes, and drift back to sleep.

27

Mama's worry lines make deep grooves in her forehead as she fixes herself some chai. I make us toast and grab the apricot preserves she likes from the fridge. When I came downstairs earlier than usual, I found her and Maryam in the kitchen. Bisma was still asleep in my bed, curled up like a kitten, and Mama said not to wake her.

"You'll be here after school for Aleeza?" Mama turns to me while she smears butter on her toast.

"Yeah."

"Thank you. I don't know what time we'll be back," Mama says. "Farah Auntie offered to come by and bring dinner tonight. She said she's cooking for us, and wouldn't take no for an answer."

"Yum." Farah Auntie's a good cook.

Mama takes a careful sip of her hot tea. It's in a mug that Aleeza painted for her at a birthday party, which is covered with cheerful orange daisies. She takes a bite of the toast, standing by the counter, and chews as she stares out the kitchen window. Mama always tells us to sit down when we eat, but I don't think she'd appreciate a reminder.

"What are they going to do at the hospital?" I ask.

"A few different tests. When we got the results from the scan, Dr. Gordon said we needed to go there for things they can't do in his office or at the radiology center. I'll keep you guys posted."

"Can I go with you?" I ask. "I can keep Bisma company."

"No, sweetie," Mama says. "You have to go to school."

"I don't have anything important," I argue.

"We don't know what's ahead." Mama frowns. "I need you in school today."

"Did you talk to Baba again?" Maryam asks. She's sitting at the table eating a fruit yogurt, and is dressed the most simply I've seen since school started. There's nothing shimmery on her eyelids or her lips, and she's wearing faded jeans and a T-shirt. I wonder if it's because she's feeling as out of sorts as I am since we heard the news about Bisma.

"I talked to him last night after everyone left."

"How is he?" I ask.

"He's upset about not being here. We at least have each other, but he's dealing with this by himself."

"I hope he can come quickly," Bisma says as she comes into the kitchen. She hugs each of us and points at me, which I interpret as a secret signal to thank me for letting her sleep in my bed last night. I point back at her. But then she comes closer and touches my shirt, and I see a gigantic toothpaste stain on it.

"I have to get the bus," Maryam says. She fixes Bisma's headband as she speaks. "Good luck today. Love you."

I run back upstairs to get my book bag and put on a clean shirt. When I go into our room, I notice Bisma has made both of the beds. She always makes hers, while I mostly forget to make mine. One of her stuffed animals, a fuzzy gray cat with blue eyes, is tucked next to my pillow.

While I'm packing my bag, I remember I never finished my math homework last night, so I scramble to complete it before I leave. Then I rush out the door to catch the bus, yelling bye on my way out. I sink into the green vinyl seat, listening to the chatter of the sixth graders in the front of the bus and a blend of music through the headphones the eighth graders are wearing in the back. When I get to school, Lily and Kayla are waiting for me in the gym. I haven't seen them since I texted them the news yesterday.

"How are you?" Kayla reaches me first, and hugs my arm. "Are you okay?"

"Yeah."

"I can't believe Bisma has cancer," Lily adds. "That's awful. I'm so sorry."

"It's a lymphoma." I decide that sounds better than cancer.

"My cousin had lymphoma a few years ago, and he's fine now," Kayla volunteers. "I think he had to have a bone marrow transplant, though. I can't remember exactly."

I don't recall her mentioning this before. Maybe she never told me, or maybe I wasn't paying attention or didn't grasp the significance back then. A bone marrow transplant sounds terrifying.

"My aunt had breast cancer, but they found it early. She's a survivor, and we do the Race for the Cure with her," Lily adds. "I know Bisma will be a survivor too."

Every year we get an e-mail from Lily's family asking

for sponsors for the race, or for people to join their team. Even though Mama always donates, I've never joined them. Now I wish I had, and I promise myself to go next time.

"My neighbor had some kind of cancer too. I remember when she got skinny and lost her hair. She wore hats, so you couldn't tell from a distance, but up close you could see she didn't have eyebrows," Kayla says.

I hadn't considered that Bisma's hair might fall out, and the idea makes my stomach twist into knots. I want my friends to stop talking about cancer. It's bad enough that it's all I've been thinking about. And while I'm sorry their family members and neighbor went through it, and am glad they are survivors, this isn't helping. Not right now.

"She had a blog on a special website where she updated people about what was happening with her," Kayla continues. "And people signed up to make meals for the family. I made lasagna one night, and she said it was the best she ever had."

A blog?

"Do you know the name of the website?" I ask.

"I think it was something 'care.' I can find it for you."

The other day Mama said she was struggling to keep up with concerned friends and teachers who keep calling and writing to ask about Bisma. Maybe this is something I could do to help.

"Thanks, guys," I say, remembering that I promised Ms. Levy I would update her on the situation. Now that I think of it, it probably would be a lot easier to do that through a website than having to talk about it over and over again.

"I'm going to find Ms. Levy. I'll see you in gym."

28

Ms. Levy isn't in her office or in the newspaper room, but I find Travis scrolling through photos on the computer from the STEAM assembly we had last week.

"Hi," he says as I walk into the room, before turning his head back to the screen.

"Hey. Is Ms. Levy here?"

"Haven't seen her."

"All right, thanks." I pause, wondering if I should go to my locker or stay here until the first bell rings, when Travis points to a photo.

"That's you."

I get closer and peer at the image and find myself in the audience, sitting with my friends on the floor in the cafeteria, laughing at something the speaker said. I'm happy in the photo, and it feels like a million years ago—not last Tuesday.

Travis continues. "Thanks for getting your articles in on time. We're printing now. Ms. Levy told me you, um, have some stuff going on."

"No problem." The last thing I want is for Travis to launch into another cancer story, so I change the subject. "How did the paper turn out?"

"Good. I like the angle you took in your article."

"You do?"

"Yeah. I haven't heard of microaggressions before."

"Microaggressions are different from flat-out racism or sexism, so people get away with them. But they're still wrong. And it's frustrating for the people who have to live with them every day," I explain.

"Yeah, I got that. From your article. It was cool." Travis spins his chair around and faces me.

"Thanks." This might be the first compliment I have ever gotten from him.

"Why did you change the focus of the article, though? Do you think you should have mentioned that to me since it wasn't what we agreed on?"

Here we go. I can tell Travis is trying to be careful with his words, and that it's a struggle for him not to blurt out exactly what he thinks the second he thinks it. It occurs to me that he and I are alike in that way. Mama always says that people who are too similar can butt heads. Until this moment, I always thought she was wrong. Shouldn't it be easier to get along with people who are like you?

"I wasn't able to find out much that was interesting when I interviewed Ali, so I decided to focus on microaggressions instead."

"He wasn't interesting?"

I think back on our conversations, and the only times he ever told me anything real was when we weren't doing an interview.

"I mean not that much."

"Thu suggested comparing his life in America to England. What happened to that?"

"He said something about how Americans use a lot of napkins. I didn't think that made a very exciting article."

Travis actually cracks a smile at that. "Nothing else?"

"Well, there was something funny about how he gets confused by things American people say. But that's way funnier when you hear him say it than it would be to read it."

Travis turns his chair back around to face the computer again.

"Well I guess it's good that you changed it, then."

"Really?"

"Yeah, I mean, if you think people want to read something that'll make them have to think twice about everything they say."

"But that's the whole—"

Travis looks over his shoulder and grins at me.

"I guess I'm getting the hang of these microaggression things," he says. It's a joke. A bad one, but a joke.

"I think you're already an expert," I shoot back with my own grin as I head to class.

29

Farah Auntie comes into the house carrying bags from the grocery store.

"I know I told your mom I was cooking dinner, but I'm in the mood to go out. How about that, girls?"

"What's that stuff for, then?" Aleeza asks.

"It's some fruit and deli meat for your lunches tomorrow. Where do you want to go?"

"Zaxby's!" Aleeza says.

"The fried chicken place?" Farah Auntie wrinkles her nose. "How about sushi? Do you girls like sushi?"

Aleeza shakes her head no, but Maryam pokes her.

"Anything you like is fine, Auntie," Aleeza says politely.

"Chinese? You like noodles?"

"We love noodles, thank you," Maryam says. "But shouldn't we wait for Mama and Bisma?"

Farah Auntie puts the bags down and turns around to face us.

"I spoke to your mom, and Bisma is going to have to stay at the hospital tonight."

"What? Why? What happened?" I ask. Mama said she would keep us updated, but I only got one text, hours ago, saying that everything was going slowly and that they were waiting for the doctor.

"She's fine, promise. They went to the emergency room this morning, since that's what the doctor told them to do. But it took hours for them to get a bed, since it was a nonemergency. They finally did a test in the ER to make sure Bisma's mass wasn't affecting her heart, which it isn't, thank God. Now they are admitting her."

"Why does she have to stay there if the test was negative?" Maryam asks.

"She needs to have a biopsy of the mass and some more tests, so it will be better for her to stay there. We want her to get the best treatment she can get, right?" As she says the last sentence, Farah Auntie sounds like she's leading a pep rally.

"What's a biopsy?" Aleeza asks.

"It's when they take a sample of something and test it," Farah Auntie explains. "That will help the doctors know better what they are dealing with."

"Oh." I can tell Aleeza doesn't understand, and I don't blame her. I don't either. "What about Mama?"

"She's going to stay with Bisma. And I'm going to stay here with you girls. That'll be okay, right?"

"Why can't Mama come home?" Aleeza asks.

"You don't want Bisma to be alone at the hospital, do you? Right. Good girl. Now, if you can help me put these things away, we can head out to eat." Farah Auntie starts to pat Aleeza on the head and doesn't seem to mind when she ducks out of the way after a second.

"What about Uncle? And Ali?" Maryam asks.

"They'll meet us at the restaurant." Auntie fills the fruit bowl in the kitchen and folds up the bag while we put the rest of the groceries away. "Let's go."

The restaurant is almost empty when we walk in, and the staff seems very excited to have us there.

"We'll have two more joining us," Farah Auntie says when we are guided to a table for four. Settled into a bigger table, we study the glossy menus.

"What do you girls like?" Auntie asks.

"Anything's fine," Maryam says.

"Noodles," Aleeza says.

"Something spicy," I add.

"Not too spicy," Aleeza corrects.

"How about some lo mein and some kung pao chicken? Do you prefer eggplant or green beans?"

"Green beans," we agree.

The restaurant door opens, and Uncle Saeed and Ali walk in. Ali's hair is wet, like he's freshly showered, and he's wearing a nice shirt tucked into his pants. Or, as he would say, trousers.

"Asalaamualaikum, girls," Uncle says. "Don't get up." He sits down next to Aleeza, and Ali sits next to Maryam.

"You look nice," Maryam says to Ali. "What's the occasion?"

"Ah, dinner? Mum always makes me dress smart for a restaurant." He scans our outfits and adds. "I guess 'you Americans' are more casual."

I'm wearing jeans and flip-flops, so I can't argue, but I make a face at the "you Americans" bit, which has become a running joke between us.

"Anything else you want to order?" Farah Auntie asks. She lists our choices so far, and the waiter writes them down. Uncle Saeed adds chicken corn soup and spring rolls.

"You hanging in there?" Uncle Saeed asks, and I

notice how white his teeth are as he puts his arm around Aleeza.

"I guess," I say.

"We're going to get through this together. All of us," he says, but none of us knows how to respond, and we end up mumbling. Sometimes pep talks can make you feel worse. It feels weird to be out like this without Bisma with us.

Uncle makes more conversation until the appetizers arrive and we can concentrate on eating. I throw a handful of crispy wonton strips into my soup as Ali and Maryam have a side conversation. I hear the name Kilbourn and figure they are talking about the science teacher, but then they continue to chat throughout dinner, and I'm sure it can't just be about that. They laugh a few times, and Ali seems relaxed and comfortable around my sister. Whatever nervousness he said he felt around her before looks like it's gone. When did this change happen?

When he catches me watching them, his lips curl up on one side. But then Ali turns his attention back to Maryam. So I turn back to my noodles and spicy beef and try to act like I don't care.

30

I'm rolling a small suitcase filled with everything Mama asked for through the halls of the hospital. Farah Auntie helped me pack it up after I got home from school and double-checked the toiletries. I begged Mama to let me bring it to the hospital so I could see Bisma, and she agreed.

But now that we've parked in the lot and are checking in at the visitor's desk, I'm nervous. The lobby is decorated more like a hotel or office building than a hospital. There's art on the walls, a flickering fireplace behind glass, and plush armchairs grouped together like a living room.

"You'll be going to the Pediatric Oncology Unit on the fourth floor," a cheerful lady with silver hair says to us, handing me a visitor's badge. "Elevator's down the hall to your right."

I try to smile at her, but it comes out more like a grimace.

"Thank you," Farah Auntie says for both of us.

We ride the elevator lost in our own thoughts. Farah Auntie is holding a bouquet of balloons for Bisma. I've got the peanut butter blondie bars Maryam made last night in a plastic container in my backpack. I added a couple of books from the library along with another card that Aleeza made. Maryam has to babysit, and Aleeza went home with a friend after school, which worked out well, since only two visitors are allowed at a time, and we didn't have to fight about who would get to come today.

The elevator doors open, and we follow the signs to the right place, where we are blocked by a nurses' station and have to check in again. A nurse makes sure that Bisma is able to receive visitors. Strangers have to give me permission to see my own sister.

We walk down the hall and knock on a door that has a sign that reads VISITORS PLEASE CLEAN HANDS BEFORE ENTERING next to a pump of antibacterial gel. Mama opens the door as I rub the gel on my palms.

"Salaams," she says, giving me a tight hug and kissing me on the head. "I missed you."

She thanks Farah Auntie for coming and for bringing me, which makes Farah Auntie scold her to stop thanking her. And then Mama moves out of the way and I see Bisma in the room, sitting on a chair next to a hospital bed.

"You came!" she says, opening her arms up for a hug.

I move in to hug her and stop midair when I notice plastic tubes coming out of one of her biceps.

"What is *that*?"

"My PICC line," Bisma says. "They put it in this morning."

It's so scary to see blood in one of the tubes and under the tape that I have to look away.

"Yikes. Did it hurt?" I ask, sitting down on the edge of the bed.

"Not too much. They put a tent over me with a hole where my arm stuck out so I couldn't see what they were doing. One of the nurses stayed on my side and held my other hand and talked to me the whole time. She was funny and told me jokes."

"What about Mama?"

"She had to wait outside because of germs."

"Wow, Bisma. You're so brave."

"I got scared when I saw some blood. But now I can't feel it."

"What's it for?"

"For the medicines I have to get. Once they figure out my cancer stage."

I can't believe Bisma is speaking so casually about cancer. I can barely say the word. She seems older and wiser in a couple of days. I hate cancer for changing her already.

"Everyone sent stuff for you." I change the subject. "Blondies from Maryam."

"Yummy."

"And you got another card from Aleeza. Here are some books I thought you'd like. A new series by that author."

"Thanks." Bisma spreads her arms again, so I give her a gentle hug, careful to avoid touching the arm with the tubes sticking out of it.

"How long do you have to be here?" I ask.

"A day or two. I think," Bisma says. "I don't want to miss too much school. Mama said she'll start collecting my work."

"Don't worry about that," I say. "Focus on getting better."

Bisma's face falls slightly when I say that, but I don't understand why. She doesn't need to think about anything other than beating cancer.

"Where does Mama sleep?" I ask.

"That sofa opens up into a bed. She says it's comfortable."

"Are you girls managing at home?" Mama comes over and stands by me and plays with my curls.

"Yeah."

"I'll try to come home in the afternoon tomorrow when Uncle stops by."

"Okay."

"Don't make too much work for Farah Auntie."

"I know."

Mama squeezes my shoulder.

"Thank you for taking care of everyone. I'm counting on you."

"Don't worry about us." I give my mom a kiss.

Farah Auntie is standing to the side, giving us space. I see her lips moving as she recites duas, and then she blows in Bisma's direction. Mama's done that for as long as I can remember—it's a tradition that I think blesses the person being blown on. I've been praying for Bisma too, every day. But I hate feeling that I could be doing more and not knowing what it is.

"Inshallah, you'll be home soon. We love you," Farah Auntie says.

"Love you too, Auntie. Thank you for the balloons."

"Ready to go?" Farah Auntie asks me. "They said to keep visits short."

I'm ready and grateful for an excuse to leave. It's hard to be in this place and see Bisma in a hospital gown.

"Will you come again?" Bisma asks.

"If you're not home first," I promise.

When we walk out of the room, a kid passes us in the hallway holding on to the hand of a nurse. He's tiny, missing his hair, and so thin he almost seems transparent. I realize he's what I was afraid to see, right now and in the future, as the hairs on my arms stand up. But the little boy flashes me a beautiful smile and continues to head to wherever he's going.

31

"This is really good." Kayla catches up to me in the hall, waving her copy of the year's first issue of the *Crossing*. "I like your article a lot. But I thought you said Ali didn't want to be in it."

"He didn't."

"Then why do you have that whole part about what his coach said about his mom?"

NO!

I snatch the paper from Kayla, which I haven't seen yet, and scan the article. There's Ali's name and his anecdote. Everything I said I wouldn't print about him is there. Printed about him. On the page. In my hand. How did this happen?

"It's the wrong version! This is the wrong version of the article!" I yell.

"What?" Kayla grabs the paper back and waves it around. "You didn't want this to print?"

"No!" My breakfast rises up into my throat.

"It's okay, it's okay," Kayla tries to reassure me. "You don't say anything bad about him, right?"

"Doesn't matter. This is terrible."

Kayla continues to speak, but I don't hear anything she says. I don't understand how this happened. I revised the article and took him out!

"I have to find Ms. Levy," I say, and I start to run down the hall to her classroom.

"You'll be late for gym," Kayla warns as I dash off faster than I ever have for a timed fifty-yard run.

Ms. Levy looks up in alarm when I burst into her classroom, breathless. Her English students are getting into their chairs and waiting for the bell to ring.

"Jameela? What are you doing here?"

"The newspaper. It's wrong. My article's wrong," I pant.

"I'm sorry, but I have to teach." Ms. Levy frowns. "And you should be in class right now. Can't this wait until lunch?"

I feel twenty sets of eyes staring at me as the bell rings, and sweat trickles down my neck. It'll have to wait, since I have no choice.

"I guess so. Can I get a pass to gym?"

32

"Calm down, Jameela." Ms. Levy is standing between Travis and me as if she is refereeing a boxing match. "It sounds like an honest mistake. Travis didn't do this on purpose."

"You sent me an e-mail saying your files were in the drive. I went to the drive, and your articles were there. So I used them." Travis repeats what he already said, this time extra slowly, like I'm a toddler.

"There were two versions of this article. You used the older one! Why didn't you check the date?"

"Why didn't you delete the old version?"

I can't answer that. The truth is that I thought it was so much better and couldn't part with it, but that's too embarrassing to admit.

"I wanted to save it in case I needed it later." That sounds reasonable, and it's mostly true. Maybe I would have been able to use it sometime in the future, if Ali let me.

"Jameela." Ms. Levy puts a hand on my shoulder. "What's the issue with this version of the article that printed? Why are you so upset about it?"

"Yeah. I don't get it," Travis adds, sounding irritated and confused at the same time. "Remember? We talked about it, and I told you I liked it."

"I thought you were talking about the new version the whole time." I sink into a chair and cradle my head with my hands.

"What's the problem with this one?" Ms. Levy asks.

"I, um." I pause, realizing that this situation makes me look horrible. I might be the worst journalist ever.

Ms. Levy and Travis both stare at me, waiting.

"Ali told me he didn't want to be in the article after I told him I was taking the microaggression angle. The new version I wrote didn't have him in it."

"But you were originally going to feature him, right?" Travis says. "He agreed. And then you interviewed him. So it's not his call what angle you decide to take."

I hadn't thought about that. It's a good point. But it doesn't apply in this case.

"Well. He didn't say that stuff about his coach and his mom when I interviewed him."

"What?" Travis seems puzzled as Ms. Levy starts to whistle under her breath, and I know she understands.

"You mean it was off the record, right?" she says.

"Yes." My voice sounds tiny.

"Oh, hon." Ms. Levy shakes her head. "You can't include something if you agree it's off the record."

"Well we didn't actually agree on it," I say.

"In that case—"

"Because it was something he told me before I knew I was going to be writing about him." I cut her off before she finishes her thought, and Ms. Levy's face falls.

"No, no, no. You don't do that." She shakes her head.

"I know." I sense her disappointment and imagine my name being forever removed from her list of potential editors in chief for next year, a giant strikethrough in permanent ink.

"So what do we do now?" Travis asks. "Is Ali mad at you?"

"I haven't seen him yet," I say. "What should I do?"

"Well." Ms. Levy chews on one of her manicured nails. "You can offer to print a correction of some kind. He could write a letter to the editor that we run. I honestly don't know. We should think it over."

I want to melt into my shoes.

"I'm sorry. I should have been more careful. Sorry for blaming you, Travis," I say.

Travis shrugs.

"Next time make sure there's one version."

"Yeah." I want to say, "Next time check the date," but I don't.

"It's a shame," Ms. Levy says. "Because you bring up an important topic, and it's a good article otherwise. You're going to have to figure out how to fix this."

The second that school is dismissed, I type a message to Ali while I walk out for the bus.

I'm so sorry. It was a mistake. Can we talk pls?

He doesn't respond.

33

Ali still hasn't texted me back by dinnertime.

One of Mama's friends, Hania Auntie, came by earlier in the afternoon with enormous aluminum trays of food. Now we have enough to feed a crowd at a dinner party, not three girls.

"What is this?" Aleeza lifts the foil off one of the trays and eyes the contents suspiciously. "Rice with peas? I hate peas."

The next tray is loaded with my favorite, keema—spiced ground beef with potatoes. And the third has chicken curry. At the moment, the sight of it makes my stomach flip. Ever since Kayla showed me the newspaper this morning, I've been queasy.

"We'll be eating this for a week," I estimate. "Maybe longer."

"It was nice of her to bring it over," Maryam says. "At least Mama doesn't have to worry about food for us. And Farah Auntie is already doing so much."

The mention of Farah Auntie makes me think of Ali again. I check my phone for the hundredth time to see if he's responded now, although he hadn't five minutes ago. It's like a mini punch to the gut when there's nothing there.

"When's Auntie getting here?" Aleeza asks.

"She's coming later," Maryam says.

"Mama said I could go to the hospital today, but no one took me," Aleeza complains.

"Bisma had her biopsy. It wasn't a good day for visitors," Maryam explains.

"But I want to see her. And Mama."

"I know. So do I. Come on—let's eat now."

We warm up individual plates in the microwave and eat in front of the TV, something that Mama would never let us do. Hania Auntie's food is tasty, and once I start eating, I feel hungry.

"I think I deserve to have a phone," Aleeza declares during a commercial for a family cell phone plan with a goofy guy in a yellow shirt.

Maryam looks up from her phone. She's managed to eat, text, and watch TV at the same time.

"You're only ten. Jam and I didn't get phones until we turned thirteen," she reminds Aleeza.

"But Mama isn't here, and I never know what's going on," Aleeza whines.

"What difference would a phone make?" I ask.

"I could text her. And Baba. And you guys."

"I'm good," I say. "I don't need you texting me."

"It's not fair," Aleeza whines. "My friends have phones, and Snapchat."

"Are you serious? Your friends have phones? Ten-year-olds? Who?" I don't believe her.

"Haley and Margaret, and other people you don't know."

"Well, they must need phones for some reason."

"They just got them. And they can do cute things on Snapchat. Like put bunny ears on people."

"You're not getting Snapchat," I warn her. "Even I don't have it yet."

"Why not?" Aleeza says. "It's like a game."

"You don't need to understand why." I point my fork at her. "You're not getting it."

"Why do you care? You don't get to decide," Aleeza starts to shriek until we hear the front door open downstairs. We gave Farah Auntie an extra key so she can come and go as she needs.

"You're both on your phones all the time. It's not fair," Aleeza quickly adds in a lower voice.

"Life isn't fair," I growl at her. "Use the home phone and stop complaining. You make everything worse."

Aleeza's eyes grow wide and start to fill up. When Farah Auntie gets to the top of the stairs, Aleeza runs over to her and hides behind her. I get up to put my plate in the sink, mumbling salaam to Farah Auntie on the way. I can hear Mama in my head saying "Be kind," but I can't be right now. I don't know how Mama controls her anger. Mine is gnawing away at my heart, making it smaller.

I head to my room and flop on the bed. Bisma's stuffed cat is lying next to my pillow, and I bury my face in it, holding back tears. When I finally get up to blow my nose, I stare at Bisma's side of the room and at her bed, made up and not slept in for the past couple of nights. It feels like she's been away for much longer, and like Baba's been away forever.

Baba.

Talking to him will make things better, like always. He can help me fix the Ali situation, or at least figure out what to do. I glance at the clock, and it's seven forty-five p.m., which means it's the middle of the night in Abu Dhabi and he's probably asleep. I send him a long text explaining how I messed up big time and that I need to talk to him when he wakes up. Next I try to FaceTime Mama, and she doesn't answer her phone either. I don't text her, since she's already dealing with so much at the hospital. The last thing I want to do is stress her out more.

I check to see if Ali has responded yet.

Nothing.

I swallow my pride and send another message.

I promise it was a mistake I wrote another version but didn't delete the old one I didn't try to go against what you wanted you have to believe me.

And then I wait.

34

I wake up when it's dark outside, lying on top of my bedspread, wearing my clothes from yesterday. That means I fell asleep without changing or brushing my teeth, but I push Uncle Saeed's warnings and visions of cavities burrowing into my teeth out of my mind. My phone is lying next to me, its battery almost dead, since I didn't recharge it in Mama's room like I'm supposed to at night. I hold my breath and check and . . . there's a message from Mama.

But nothing from Ali.

Mama's message is a long paragraph about how she's sorry she missed my call, and that Bisma handled her biopsy like a champ, misses me, and was sending love. She also reminded me to take out the garbage, which I hope Maryam did before she went to bed, so I don't have to. I write Mama a quick reply and then crawl under my covers.

It's only 5:39 a.m., but as I try to go back to sleep, random thoughts swirl through my head like glitter in the snow globe on Bisma's nightstand. In a matter of weeks, Baba got a new job and moved across the world, Bisma got sick and has to be in the hospital, and I messed up everything with Ali and the paper. How did my whole life get turned upside down so quickly?

As my throat starts to tighten, I get out of bed, wash my face, and brush my teeth. Then I go downstairs, pour myself a big bowl of cereal, and find the laptop. I remember that Kayla sent me the name of a website to check out for Bisma: CaringBridge. The site says you can set up a private web page in three minutes where you can keep a journal, get comments from people who follow you, organize help with meals and rides, and more.

Mama said she's had to turn friends from the community away from the hospital, since the visitor policy is so strict. It's super nice that everyone is offering to make and drop off food, but we'll run out of space in the fridge, and our stomachs, if people bring over as much as Hania Auntie did.

I go through the steps to create a profile for Bisma

and then start to draft the first journal entry. I write about how Bisma had a lump in her neck that hurt, how she went to the doctor, and how he thought she had an infection. I continue to explain how she took antibiotics but they didn't work, and the doctor worried when she developed a second lump then. I detail how she went for a scan, and they found a mass in her chest and sent her to the hospital for more tests. Getting admitted to the hospital, having a PICC line put in, needing a biopsy—I include everything that I know about and can remember. But as I write out the facts, I'm struck by how much more to the story there is that I don't know.

How does it *feel* to be the person who learns she has cancer? What is it like to know that your life has changed in an instant? How do you absorb the worry on your mother's face? How can you process this news when your father is across the world? What do you think about when other people are praying for you? What do you learn about yourself in these moments?

I start to compile a huge list of questions for Bisma like I do when I'm going to write an article and do an interview. But it occurs to me that I'm acting like a journalist again—and I clearly failed at that already. So I delete the questions, close the lid of the computer, and start to get ready for school. It's only while I'm getting dressed that I start to yawn and feel drowsy, or "knackered" as Ali would say. That is, if he were talking to me.

35

"This is a good time for us to have a conversation about ethics in journalism," Ms. Levy announces at the start of our meeting. She stands at the whiteboard, where she's written out four points in blue marker.

I duck my head and pretend to search for my pencil on the floor, but can feel everyone's eyes on me.

"To be clear, this isn't to blame anyone for anything," she continues. "It's important to keep these points in mind as we move forward with our remaining issues of the *Crossing* this year."

Travis is standing next to Ms. Levy like he's her assistant and nodding like a bobblehead in his eagerness to show how much he approves.

"Journalists and the field of journalism have been

under attack in recent years, accused of telling lies and spreading their own agendas rather than being objective. In a few cases, it's unfortunately true. But, as we've talked about before, a strong, independent media is critical to democracy. And as future journalists, it's more important than ever to always follow these four basic principles of ethics."

Ms. Levy starts with the first point, *Seeking Truth and Reporting It*, and delves into sources, how we get news, being careful making promises, and more. I see everyone's bored expressions and feel guilty that this entire lecture is because of me, no matter what Ms. Levy says. I'm certain everyone in the room has heard about my mistake by now.

"Does this mean that if someone says something to you, and it's not officially an interview, you can never put it in an article?" Callie asks what everyone is probably thinking.

"Not necessarily. But you need to ask them, 'Can I quote you?' Right?" Ms. Levy says.

"Got it." Callie nods.

"Like you always ask before you record a conversation or take notes," Travis adds.

Ms. Levy goes on to talk about *Acting Independently*, which I know I did. No one paid me to write my story or influenced me. If anything, I'm the person who gets in trouble more than I'd like for acting independently.

"What about ads in the paper?" Lynn asks. "Couldn't companies putting ads in papers control what people write about?"

"They never should," Ms. Levy says. "Or that would be unethical. These are great questions."

Next Ms. Levy talks about *Minimizing Harm*, which makes me squirm in my seat as I think about the harm I caused Ali. Whether or not I thought what he said was something worth publishing, the fact that his words were printed without his permission broke the rules of journalism, and his trust—even if it was by accident. I don't know how or when he will ever want to share anything with me again.

The last point Ms. Levy makes is about *Being Accountable and Transparent*.

"This includes acknowledging mistakes and finding the best way to correct or clarify things when necessary." Even though she said this conversation wasn't because of me, Ms. Levy glances in my direction.

"I'm working on it," I respond. "I just don't know how yet."

I'm surprised when, as the meeting wraps up, Thu comes up to me while everyone else rushes out of the room to get ready for class or meet friends.

"I thought your article was great, ethics aside," she says.

"Thanks. I think," I reply.

"I mean, the topic is something that no one ever talks about at school, but we totally need to. People say things that I guess are microaggressions about being Asian that really hurt sometimes."

"I wanted to call them out. It's not okay to say things like that." I still feel like crap, but I appreciate Thu's effort.

"Maybe this helps to make people be more thoughtful about what they say than before," she adds.

"Maybe."

"Of course, that would mean they'd have to actually read the paper," Thu sighs.

"True."

"But it was good. I'm glad you wrote it." Thu hands me her copy of the paper, and I hold on to it, since I forgot to save one of this issue. I didn't even want one until now.

"Thanks," I say. "For real."

"No problem. Sorry about what happened with the version mix-up, though. That sucks."

"Yeah," I agree.

It really does.

36

I open the front door and find Farah Auntie standing there with her overnight bag, purse, and a reusable shopping bag.

"Asalaamualaikum. Sorry, I couldn't find the key in my purse. I have too much junk in here." Farah Auntie hands me her bag. "Could you take this upstairs to your mom's room for me?"

"Waalaikum asalaam," I reply. "Sure."

"Nazish Auntie made you guys some meatballs and sauce. I need to boil the pasta. That work for dinner?"

"That sounds great." I pause. "Are Uncle and Ali going to come too?" I try to sound casual and not like I'm dying to know.

"I don't think so. Not for dinner." Farah Auntie pulls

out her phone and swipes through it. She doesn't seem to notice anything strange about how I sound or sense my disappointment at her response.

Maryam comes into the family room and offers to help Farah Auntie fix dinner. Aleeza's sitting on the floor as she empties her take-home folder and holds up a permission slip for a field trip her grade is having to the Georgia Aquarium.

"Who's going to sign this for me?" she asks.

"I'm sure I can do that," Farah Auntie says.

"But we have to pay seventeen dollars."

"That's fine, love. I'll write you a check."

"I miss Mama. And Baba. And Bisma. Why can't they come home?" Aleeza drops her head and sniffles. For a change, I'm almost glad to see her eyes well up, because I feel exactly the same way she does. When Aleeza notices she doesn't have a bigger audience, she dries her eyes and goes back to her folder.

I think about what my mom said a while ago about Aleeza being the youngest and being patient with her. I know that I haven't been.

"Hey, Aleeza. Let's make something together," I offer after a moment.

"What?" She looks up in surprise.

"I don't know. Bisma liked the card you made her.

But wouldn't it be cool to make her a big sign?"

"To hang on the wall?" Aleeza's face brightens. "Like a welcome-home sign?"

"Yeah." I was thinking of a poster for her hospital room. But a welcome-home sign definitely sounds more optimistic.

Aleeza runs to the cupboard and pulls out her markers.

"I don't have any big paper," she says.

"We can tape regular paper together. Let's put a letter on each page."

"Good idea!" Aleeza agrees. This is one of the first times in a long time I'm doing something with her other than fight, and it feels good. The scent of pasta fills the room, and my stomach growls. No matter what's going on or how strange life feels, my body knows it's time for dinner.

"You guys want garlic bread?" Maryam sticks her head out of the kitchen.

"Yes!" Aleeza and I say in unison. I make a *W* in a rainbow design, and Aleeza creates an *E* in a cool tie-dye pattern. Aleeza's tongue sticks out slightly while she concentrates on coloring, like Baba's does whenever he works with his hands on something.

"Let's eat, guys." Maryam calls us, and we pause to join her and Auntie. I dig into the pots on the stove first, loading my plate with spaghetti and topping it with plenty of sauce. I'm in the middle of eating, twirling noodles around my fork, when the doorbell rings and startles me. It's already dark outside, and we aren't expecting anyone else.

"I'll get it." Aleeza drops her fork with a clang, pops out of her seat, and starts to run downstairs.

"Wait!" I command. "Don't open the door to strangers."

"It's my friend stopping by," Farah Auntie says, wiping her mouth on a napkin. "Go ahead and open it, sweetie."

Aleeza turns back to me from the doorway of the kitchen. "It's fine. Go." I urge her.

When I hear screams a few seconds later, I drop my own fork and run down the stairs to see what's going on. Maryam is a few steps behind me.

When I get to the final step, I let out a shout too.

Baba is standing in the doorway wearing a gigantic smile and holding Aleeza in his arms.

"Baba! You came!" I jump up and down and clap my hands as my father leans over to kiss me on the forehead. He beckons Maryam, who is frozen in disbelief, to come closer.

I move to let Maryam hug Baba, and spot Ali standing behind him.

"Surprise," he says softly. "This is what I was busy doing."

Without thinking, I throw my arms around him and give him an enormous hug. "It's the best surprise ever! Thank you so much!" I say. When I pull away, Ali blushes, and I feel my cheeks heat up too.

"Sorry," I mumble. "I didn't mean to throw myself at you."

Baba sets Aleeza down and moves Ali in front of him, placing both hands on his shoulders.

"This guy," Baba says proudly. "He found my flights for me. Uncle helped me sort through my contract and request leave. I wasn't sure until the last minute that I would be able to come. I'm so grateful to each of you." Baba points to Farah Auntie, who is hanging out on the stairs, beaming. Uncle walks in with Baba's suitcase and greets us.

"Are you back for good?" Aleeza asks Baba.

"Not yet," he says. "But I'm working on it. I need to be here with Bisma and all of you right now."

"How long will you stay?" she asks.

"At least a couple weeks."

Maryam turns to Ali. "I can't believe you kept this a secret from us."

"It was your dad's idea. I was afraid I was going to let it slip," he replies.

"It's an awesome surprise," I offer quickly, looking at Ali to see how he reacts.

He gives me a slight nod of acknowledgment and then turns to Aleeza, who is tugging on his shirt.

Now I know why I couldn't get ahold of Baba, or why he didn't respond to me. He was on a plane for the past twenty hours. But he's home, at least for now. And even if I don't know what's going on with Ali, it's amazing how much better I feel already.

37

Baba washes up, eats a few bites, and heads straight to the hospital with Uncle Saeed. I reheat my plate and finish eating and then wash the dishes, while Ali scarfs down the rest of the pasta and meatballs, plus a few pieces of garlic bread.

"Maryam, can you help me fix your parents' bed?" Farah Auntie asks. "I'm not staying here tonight. One of your parents will be back."

"But you packed a bag," I remind her. "Why'd you bring it if you're not staying?"

"I wanted to be convincing," Farah Auntie confesses. "That bag has my dry cleaning in it."

We laugh with her, and Ali gives his aunt a high five to celebrate pulling off the surprise. Mama always says that Farah Auntie and Uncle Saeed more than make up for the family we don't have in Georgia. I've never felt it more than now as I think about how much time, energy, and love they've given to us so freely, without asking for anything in return.

When Maryam and Auntie go up to change the linens, and Aleeza reluctantly follows to get ready for bed, I turn to Ali, who is leaning back in his chair, acting slightly pained from eating so much.

I decide I might as well get right into it.

"Did you get my texts?" I ask.

"Yeah." Ali twists the edge of his napkin until it's pointy.

"I'm so sorry about the article. You have to believe it was a mistake."

Ali stares at me, but I can't read his eyes or tell how upset he is.

"Listen," I proceed like he's very upset. "I changed the story and took you completely out. I'll show it to you. But when I submitted it, I didn't delete the old version, and so Travis published the wrong one. And also—" I'm saying everything quickly, and Ali waves his hands and shakes his head like he doesn't understand. I forget he isn't used to American accents sometimes.

"Hold on," he says. "You're saying this is Travis's fault?"

"No, no. It's my fault." I correct myself. "I should have been more careful."

"And?" Ali raises his eyebrows like he's waiting for more.

"And . . ." I pause as I think about everything that happened. "And I should have kept the focus of the article on you."

"And?" I try to read Ali's eyes, and they aren't dark and cold like I expect. Instead they are almost . . . amused. Like he's enjoying watching me squirm. I bite my lip and try to keep my cool, remembering that Ali has a right to act this way.

"And I shouldn't have forced your private life into the issue I wanted to cover. I was wrong," I say.

"Is that it?" he asks.

"Well, I wanted to write an article that would make my dad really proud of me. He always makes a big deal about my writing, but I never wrote about anything that mattered to anyone other than my family, or that would make a difference in the real world, you know?"

Ali pulls off a tiny piece of the napkin and rolls it into a ball, and I feel my heart pounding in my throat.

"I didn't have a present for him when he left, and I told myself this was for him," I continue.

When he looks at me, Ali's eyes are softer.

"All right," he finally says quietly as he gets up and throws the napkin in the trash.

I'm confused. Does that mean he's forgiving me?

"If it makes you happy, I probably won't get to be editor in chief now," I add after a moment.

Ali raises his eyebrows again. "Because of me? No, no, no. That doesn't make me happy. The world needs you to do your journalism thing."

"The world needs you" is something Baba has said to me for years. He didn't respond to the twenty or so texts I sent him, since he was flying, but must have read them when he landed.

"What did my father say to you on the drive home?" I ask.

"Just how proud he is of you, and how passionate you are about writing the truth, and how your heart is in the right place. Blah blah blah." Ali pauses.

"Is that why you're not angrier?"

"I'm plenty angry," Ali says. "At first I thought you printed that stuff on purpose, when you knew I didn't want you to. But then I didn't think you'd do that."

"I wouldn't," I insist.

"I saw your messages about it being a mistake, but I wasn't ready to talk to you," Ali continues. "Then your dad asked me to go easy on you. He said you forgot to e-mail your article to him. Plus everyone is upset and overwhelmed about Bisma, which I understand."

"And so?" I ask hesitantly.

"So, I guess I'm over it."

"Really?"

"Yeah." Ali nods. "I think so."

"I'll make it up to you," I offer. "What can I do?"

Ali scratches his head.

"Throw yourself at me again." He winks. "I kind of liked it."

"Very funny," I say, as my face warms up. But as we walk out of the kitchen, I can't stop smiling.

38

The welcome-home sign is hanging in the family room, along with some of the flowers and balloons Baba brought back from the hospital last night. After visiting Bisma, he returned and passed out. We all woke up late this Saturday morning, and Maryam, Aleeza, and I tried to stay quiet and let him sleep longer.

Mama called an hour ago to say that Bisma was coming home today, and since then it's been like we're preparing for a party. Maryam started making blueberry muffins in the kitchen. Aleeza and I have been cleaning the house, although she's better at making a mess. At least she's trying.

"Use less of that stuff." I cough as she sprays wood polish on the coffee table. "That's too much. And you're leaving streaks. You have to rub it in."

Aleeza doesn't argue. She's in a good mood and didn't grumble when I said we had to get the house ready for Bisma. We hung up the sign we finished this morning. In the end, we cut paper into the shape of banner flags like Aleeza suggested and strung them on a long piece of red ribbon. It's much nicer than I imagined it would be. Aleeza said we make a good team and that I'm not as terrible at art as I thought I was. She might be right.

"Good morning." Baba comes down the stairs in sweats, his hair sticking out in different directions. His face is full of stubble.

"Can you please make me some chai in a travel mug?" he asks me. "I'm going to shower and go pick up Mama and Bisma. She's being discharged at noon."

"Sure," I say. "Do you want a bagel?"

"That'd be great."

It's only been five days since I shared toast with Mama the day she left for the hospital, but it feels like forever. So much has changed.

We have to wait for hours for Baba to return with Mama and Bisma. Baba calls to say that the discharge process is taking a long time, and that he and Mama had to learn how to flush Bisma's PICC line. Which means Mama had to learn. Baba studies diseases and can talk at the dinner table about the most disgusting symptoms, but he's super squeamish around needles and blood. Whenever my sisters and I have gotten a cut or scrape, Mama's been the one to clean it up for us. Once, when Baba tried to donate blood at a Red Cross drive at the mosque, he got woozy and almost fainted.

Now Bisma is finally home, sitting on the couch, looking exhausted but comfortable. Maryam and Aleeza cried when they saw her PICC line, and Aleeza still seems scared to touch her or to get too close.

"After the tests and scans, the doctors think Bisma has stage two bulky Hodgkin's lymphoma," Mama explains. She's sitting on the opposite end of the sofa, and she grabs a throw blanket and drapes it over Bisma's and her own legs.

"Is that . . . good news?" Maryam is seated on the carpet near Bisma's head.

"Well, it's a very treatable form of lymphoma. So, yes, that's the good news. But she has to go through four rounds of chemotherapy starting Monday."

Chemotherapy. That's almost as scary a word as cancer. I envision the little boy from the hospital and wonder if he had it.

"What about your . . . hair?" I ask.

Bisma touches one of the long curls that frame her face. "My favorite nurse said I should cut it short now.

She said it'll be easier for me when it starts to fall out."

"So it's going to fall out? Like all of it?" Aleeza asks.

"Probably."

"I think a pixie cut would be cute on you," Maryam says. "You totally have the bone structure to pull it off."

She starts to scroll through her phone and pulls up a few images.

"Maybe you could do something like that?" Maryam shows Bisma and the rest of us a photo of a young actress whose name I don't remember.

"Maybe. That's nice," Bisma says, but as she hands Maryam the phone back, I see the regret in her eyes. She doesn't want to lose her hair any more than we want to see it go.

"Where do you do the chemotherapy?" I ask.

"Bisma picked the clinic instead of staying at the hospital, so we'll be home as long as it goes well," Mama says.

"What about school?" Aleeza asks. "Will you be able to go?"

"I don't know yet. We have to talk to my teachers and see what I can do so I don't get too behind."

"I need to respond to her teachers and everyone who's been asking after Bisma and offering to help," Mama sighs. "I didn't have a good signal at the hospital. And honestly, I got tired of repeating myself."

That reminds me. I grab the laptop and log in to the CaringBridge site. In the profile I created for Bisma, I added her school photo from last year and one of us sisters from Eid. In the end, I wrote a simple journal entry, welcoming people to Bisma's page. I left out specific details about the disease but invited everyone to join her on the journey to fight cancer and to leave comments and messages of support.

"Check this out." I show Bisma and Mama. "If you share the link, your friends can follow you and find out what's going on without calling or texting."

"This is fantastic," Mama says as she scrolls through the page. "Do you think you could help me keep up with the journal?"

"I'll write it."

"Oh, would you? That would be so great." Mama seems more excited about it now.

"There's a section to coordinate help like rides or meals. You can ask for things we need, and people can sign up."

"This is great. You know I don't like to ask for favors. But so much of the burden has fallen on Farah and Saeed," Mama says as she clicks through the section.

"You would do the same for them," Baba says from the dining table, where he's fixing his glasses with a repair kit and the tiniest screwdriver I've ever seen. "Plus, you heard what the doctors said during discharge. This is a long road, and it's no time to be formal or refuse help. They advised us to get as much support as we can."

"I guess," Mama agrees. My mother is usually the one cooking and doing things for other people.

"Should I make the site live?" I ask. "Do you like it, Bisma? I'll write the updates myself, or we can do them together if you want."

"I like it." Bisma thanks me with her eyes, but there's seriousness in her demeanor that wasn't there before. Even though she's sitting in front of me, it feels like part of my little sister didn't return from the hospital.

39

The stylist, wearing a name tag that says RENEE, swivels Bisma around in the chair to face us. Bisma's long locks are in piles on the floor, and her new, cropped hair is styled with gel.

"How do you like it?" Renee asks.

"I don't know." Bisma frowns at her reflection in the handheld mirror Renee gave her to view the back of her head. "I look so . . . different."

"You look great," I assure her. "So great you're making me want to cut off my hair too. Get up. Let me in that seat."

"No way." Bisma grimaces. "Your hair is perfect the way it is!"

"You look awesome," Maryam reassures Bisma. "Promise."

"It's cute," Aleeza agrees. She's been sitting on the side, doodling in a sketchbook while we waited. "Can we get ice cream now?"

When we're hanging out on the benches outside of Bruster's, I take a photo of Bisma in her new hairdo, holding a waffle cone of mint chocolate chip ice cream, and show it to her.

"That good? I'm going to post it in the journal with today's entry."

"I guess so." Bisma peers at the photo. "No one will recognize me."

"Sure they will," I say.

"You can add this, too, if you want," Aleeza says, showing us the sketch she was working on. It's a rough crayon portrait of Bisma that resembles something a fashion designer might draw, with a caption: *STAY STRONG*. I'm seriously impressed.

"Whoa! That's so cool," Maryam says. "Don't you think, Bisma?"

"Yeah." Bisma tries to smile.

"The post is ready then, Mama, unless you want to add anything?" I ask.

"Remind me when we get home. You girls ready to

go? Can we stop at Target? I need to grab a few things."

Stopping at Target turns into full-fledged grocery shopping as Mama disappears into the food aisles. I follow her while my sisters search for items on a list that Bisma's nurses said could come in handy during her chemotherapy infusions.

Mama picks up a loaf of broad and reads the ingredients.

"I want us to start eating healthier," she says. "Do we have oatmeal at home?"

"Are you making porridge?" I ask.

Mama smiles. "Are we calling it that now?"

"I guess. Can I ask you a question?"

"Sure."

"If Baba doesn't go back and finish the whole job in Abu Dhabi, are we going to have enough money for our house? And to pay for all of Bisma's treatment?"

Mama stops rolling the cart and looks at me.

"Jam." She frowns. "Have you been worrying about money on top of everything else?"

"A little."

Mama's shoulders slump, and it looks like she shrunk an inch.

"I'm so sorry, baby. You do not need to be thinking about this." She puts her hands out and grabs mine. "We will be fine, inshallah. Baba already has some good leads for jobs here, and our insurance is going to cover Bisma's treatment."

"Okay."

"I didn't realize that you were anxious. I should have paid more attention. I was busy working extra hours, and then with everything with Bisma and with your dad—"

"It's fine. Honest. I just wanted to know."

Mama bites her lip and then gives me a long hug, right there in front of the potato rolls.

"You can always come to me with whatever is on your mind, okay? Baba and I don't talk about money matters in front of you guys so you won't worry. Things were pretty tight when he was out of work, but we're managing now."

She starts to roll the cart, then halts and looks at me again.

"In the future, if you're worried, come to me. I'll tell you what's going on. You've proven you can handle it."

"You'll tell me everything?" I ask.

"Well . . ." Mama smiles. "Within reason. Come on—let's find the others."

My sisters are in the candy aisle, but as we approach them, Mama remembers we need eggs and goes back to get them. She tells us to meet her at the checkout line.

"Life Savers or Jolly Ranchers?" Aleeza holds up both in Bisma's direction. "The list says these are good for the bad taste you might get in your mouth."

"Jolly Ranchers," Bisma chooses.

Maryam grabs some trail mix and granola bars.

"Like these healthy snacks to munch on during your treatment?"

"Sure."

As we walk toward the registers, I find a soft, fuzzy blanket in a clearance aisle, and Aleeza spots a stuffed llama and hugs it.

"What about this? He's so cute. And he can keep you company."

It goes into the cart too.

"You don't have to get me all this," Bisma says quietly. "It's too much."

"No it isn't," I say. "Remember you said you were bored at the hospital? You're going to be sitting for hours. What else would you like?"

Mama walks up to us.

"Where's Bisma?"

"I'm right here," Bisma replies. Mama had looked right past her.

"Right. There you are!" Mama tousles her hair. "I'm not used to this yet. But I will be!"

Bisma acts glum as we leave the store but remembers to thank Mama for the things.

"Tired?" Mama asks her.

"Yeah."

When we get home, Bisma and Aleeza watch TV on the couch. I collect a bunch of other things into an old backpack for Bisma. I add my iPod, where I downloaded some of Bisma's favorite music, and my headphones, since hers broke. I throw in a deck of cards, a book of magic tricks that I was trying to learn a while ago and never mastered, and a sudoku book I didn't have the patience for either. When the bag is stuffed with things to keep her busy during chemo, I'm glad I have something for her, but it's not enough.

I get to go to school tomorrow and see my friends and be in class and worry about my math test and work on the school newspaper. Meanwhile, Bisma is going to be sitting with a needle in her arm, inviting medicines into her body to kill cancer cells.

I've been praying so hard for her to get better. But there has to be something more I can do. I can't let her fight this battle alone.

40

Cancer sucks. I hate seeing what it is doing to my sister. It's the second week of her first chemo cycle, and Bisma is wearing a surgical mask, curled up in my chair with her new fuzzy blanket, half-asleep, watching *The Incredibles*. I knew chemo was going to be tough, and we were warned about what it would be like, but it's much worse than I imagined.

Bisma's nauseated, and her stomach hurts a lot. She's so weak that it's hard for her to stand up for more than a few minutes. It's been exactly the same temperature in the house, but she randomly feels hot and then freezing cold. And she hasn't been able to go to school for the past two weeks.

The mask is to protect her from the germs we have.

Aleeza has the sniffles, so she's been instructed to stay far away from Bisma. Since Bisma's immune system is weak, she can't afford to get sick, and if she gets a fever, she'll have to go to the hospital. None of us wants that to happen, and Mama yelled at Aleeza for sneezing into her hands. That made Aleeza cry, of course.

I thought about what Mama had said to me about how hard she works to keep her temper in check, but it slipped out anyway when she was worried about Bisma. I've been watching her more closely since the day she told me about her struggle with her emotions and feel more connected to her than ever. I hope that I can keep it together and be as calm as my mother one day.

"Do you want a smoothie?" Baba asks, but Bisma shakes her head.

"I'm going to take a nap," she says, switching off the TV.

Since Baba's been home for the past two weeks, he's been taking turns driving Bisma to her appointments and making green shakes and whatever else he can think of to entice Bisma to keep eating. The rest of the time he's been in meetings and talking on the phone. He has to go back to Abu Dhabi for a few weeks to wrap things up, but then he's decided he's going to take a job here, even if it's not exactly what he wants to do or as good as the one he has now.

I follow Bisma into our room, and she turns around and says, "I'm okay, Jam. You don't have to watch me like I'm going to break."

"Fine. I'm going to go read," I say. "Call me if you need anything."

"Can you wake me up when Ali gets here?" Bisma asks.

"He's coming?"

"Yeah. He said he wanted to visit, and Mama said he could."

I've seen Ali at school a few times and said hi to him in the halls. He and Uncle and Auntie came over a couple of times for short visits, but it's been to check in on Bisma, drop something off, or help out. It's like all our lives have been taken over by cancer and chemo in one way or another. It's what we talk about and think about, more than anything else.

When Ali arrives, I open the door. He's got his backpack on, which he removes along with his shoes at the door. Then he takes a brown paper bag out of his backpack.

"Hey," he says. "How are you doing?"

"Good. Bisma's napping. She said to wake her up when you got here. Should I?"

"If you think it's all right."

I lead Ali upstairs to the family room, and then continue up the second flight to my bedroom alone. Bisma is already awake, lying in her bed reading a pile of cards she got from school.

"Ali's here," I say. "Do you want to come down? And put on your mask?"

"Can he come up?" she asks. "I'm not wearing the mask in here."

I survey our room. Of course my bed isn't made, so I quickly throw my bedspread over the lumpy sheets. I dump everything on my nightstand into the top drawer and clear our desk chair of laundry that I've been meaning to put away.

"Now he can." I'm out of breath. "Ali? Do you mind coming up here?" I yell.

Ali comes in a minute later, holding the bag, which he hands to Bisma.

"You have no idea what I went through to get these," he says. "If this doesn't cure you, I don't know what will."

Bisma takes the bag.

"What is it?" she asks, peering inside.

"Only the best chocolate Britain has to offer."

"Toblerone?" I guess.

"Shame on you," Ali scoffs. "Now you don't get any."

"Maltesers?" Bisma reads the name on the bag. "What are they?"

"It's a crunchy chocolate ball that melts in your mouth."

Bisma tears the bag open and tries one.

"It's really good." She passes me the bag, and I pop one in my mouth.

"Mmm. It's like a Whopper, but—" I barely have the words out when Ali snatches the bag away.

"How dare you!" He acts horrified. "This is no measly Whopper. No more for you."

"You didn't let me finish. It's like a Whopper but BETTER."

"That's more like it." Ali hands me the bag back. "So this is your room?" I feel exposed as his eyes take in our private space.

"Which is your favorite?" he asks Bisma, pointing to the pile of stuffed toys on her bed.

"This one." Bisma holds up a well-loved lamb that used to be white but is a grimy shade of gray now.

"Aww, how cute." Ali takes it, shoves it under his shirt, and stands up. "Okay, gotta go."

"Noo!" Bisma squeals. "You can't take him!"

"Fine." Ali tosses it back to her. "But you have to let me borrow one to keep me company until I visit next time. You choose which one."

Bisma thinks hard, trying to decide which animal she can part with In the end, she picks a monkey holding a banana.

"Perfect. I shall call him Prince Cecil Melvin Hartfordshire the Flea Picker."

Bisma giggles and pops another Malteser in her mouth. She hasn't looked this relaxed in weeks.

"So what next?" Ali asks. "Do you want to watch a movie or play Would You Rather again?"

"I was watching *The Incredibles* before I napped. Do you want to see that, and play a game after?" Bisma offers.

"Perfect. But I have one question that's burning now."

"What?"

"Would you rather have cancer *or* swim in a pool filled with cat urine?"

"Eww!" Bisma laughs, and I marvel at Ali's charm and ability to make everything seem normal. Even cancer.

41

When Maryam, Mama, and Aleeza come home, they insist Ali stay for dinner. Ali keeps his attention on Bisma the whole time, except for when Aleeza interrupts. He doesn't talk to Maryam or me much, but the fact that Bisma is genuinely smiling and giggling for the first time since her diagnosis isn't lost on any of us.

After we eat, Ali clears his throat.

"I have some good news." His eyes are dancing.

"Your mom is coming!" Aleeza yells.

"Thanks for spoiling my announcement," Ali laughs. "But, yes. Mum and Zoya will be here in a couple weeks."

"Subhanallah!" Mama claps her hands. "I can't wait to see them."

"Me too," I add.

"Where will they stay? Can they stay with us?" Aleeza asks.

"With Auntie and Uncle for now. Until we get our own place. But we'll visit you."

"That's so great," Maryam says. "You must be so relieved."

"I am," Ali says. "It feels like ages."

Uncle Saeed texts to say he'll be here to pick him up in five minutes, so Ali thanks Mama for dinner and says bye to my sisters, and I walk him downstairs.

"Thanks for coming," I say as Ali puts his shoes on. "You cheered Bisma up."

"My pleasure. I'll be back to return Prince Cecil soon." Ali holds up the monkey and bounces him on both knees like a soccer ball.

"Don't forget."

"You know . . ." Ali holds Cecil under his arm. "When my dad died, I felt like people didn't know how to act around me. It made it harder."

"How?"

"They acted like I was broken, or like we weren't allowed to laugh anymore. My neighbor was the only one who understood. He was sad for me. I knew that. But he also came over and chilled with me."

"Like you did today."

"Yeah. I don't want Bisma to feel like she *is* her cancer. Or that we only see her as a sick person."

I think about how I've been treating Bisma, and that's exactly what I've been doing.

"You're totally right," I say, swallowing hard.

Ali smiles. "How hard was it for you to say that?"

"It wasn't that bad. Maybe I'm getting used to it." I smile back. Something's been on my mind ever since the day Ali told us about his dad and how he wasn't home when he had his heart attack, so I decide to bring it up.

"Can I ask you something personal?" I ask.

"Are you going to publish it in the school paper?" Ali folds his arms across his chest.

"No."

"In the national paper?"

"No!"

"Wait, don't tell me, on . . . *social media*?"

"Of course not!"

"All right, then go ahead."

"Do you think maybe you don't want to play soccer anymore because you were with your team when your dad . . ." I gulp. "When he, you know, went to the hospital?"

"What are you on about?" Ali's forehead wrinkles as he listens.

"I don't know. Do you think you maybe blame soccer, or feel guilty about it?"

Ali looks stunned, and my heart beats faster. The last thing I want to do is upset him again, but I think he might have given up something he loves for the wrong reason. He stares at me for a second and considers what I said.

"It's possible," he finally says. "I hadn't thought of that."

"I don't think you should give up on soccer because of what happened. It's not your fault." I could say more, but don't want to push it.

"Duly noted." Ali ducks to tie his shoelaces, and I can't see his face or try to read his reaction. Before I have a chance to say anything else, I hear Uncle Saeed tap his horn twice.

"My chariot awaits me," Ali says as he straightens. "Prince Cecil and I bid thee farewell."

Ali opens the door, winks at me, and leaves. I exhale slowly, relieved that he isn't upset at me for saying what I think and grateful for his visit.

I spend the rest of the evening thinking about how I've been treating Bisma and what she needs, and coming up with a plan.

42

"I want to take it all off," Bisma says. "It's grossing me out to have it come out in clumps."

Now that it's almost the end of her first chemo cycle, Bisma's hair is patchy in areas.

"Are you sure?" Mama looks hesitant. "I can take you back to Renee. Or do you want to wait a bit?"

"Can we go today, or tomorrow?" Bisma asks. "I want to go to school, but not like this."

Bisma hasn't been back to school since her diagnosis, but she's slowly getting her strength back. This past week she had a couple of friends visit and FaceTimed her class. But once she started perking up and finally seeming more like herself, her hair began to fall out.

I've been trying to treat Bisma as normally as

possible and stop myself from hovering over her and talking about being sick. I spent time researching ways to support people living with cancer and learned about a walk being held by the Leukemia & Lymphoma Society in Atlanta in a few weeks called Light the Night. Bisma registered, and now we're going to try to raise money for it. We're working on her fund-raising page together, and it's been nice to see Bisma get excited about something after a long time.

"Let me call Renee and see if she's available for a haircut." Mama goes into the kitchen, and my sisters and I circle Bisma, as if we're creating a shield around her and the prospect of her without any of her hair.

"Are you okay?" Maryam puts her arm around Bisma.

"I'm fine. I've been so worried about this happening. But I'm ready for it to be over. And it's just hair, right?" Bisma seems confident. "Inshallah, it grows back quickly."

Bisma sounds so mature it's disconcerting. While we were working on the blog, I couldn't shake the feeling that my baby sister has been snatched by aliens and replaced by a mini grown-up.

"Are you going to wear a hat to school?" Aleeza asks.

"I don't know. Maybe sometimes."

"Renee can take you at the salon in an hour," Mama says, coming out of the kitchen.

"I'll take her," Baba offers.

"Are you sure?" Mama says.

"I'm sure. It's my turn, and I want to be there."

"Can I go with you?" I ask Bisma. "Let's document this moment for the blog."

"Sure."

No one else asks to join us. I honestly don't think they want to see this happen. But watching Bisma's hair get buzzed off doesn't end up being as traumatic as I expected—at least for her. She seems far more relaxed than last time, and chats with Renee like she's getting a regular trim. Baba takes it pretty hard, though. I see him looking away and biting his nails nervously.

When Renee's done, Bisma runs her hand over her smooth head.

"It's like an egg," she giggles.

"You're beautiful," Baba corrects. He blows his nose and gazes at Bisma with a wistful mix of love and pride.

"That you are, love," Renee agrees before she blows stray hairs off Bisma's neck with a hair dryer. "The focus is on your gorgeous face now."

"Thank you." Bisma stands up after Renee removes the cape. "Ready to go?"

"Not yet," I say. "I'm next."

"Very funny. That's what you said last time."

"I'm serious this time." I sit in the swivel chair while Renee stands back and waits to see if the cape is going around me or not. "I want Renee to cut it all off."

"What?" Bisma's hand goes over her mouth. "Why?"

"I'm donating my hair to Wigs for Kids. I checked the different places that take hair, and these guys focus on kids with cancer. I have twelve inches I can give them."

"What did Mama and Baba say?"

"They said it's up to me. Right, Baba?" A few days ago Baba spotted me reading about people who either shave their heads in solidarity with loved ones who have cancer or donate hair when I was doing my research. The more I read up about donating hair, the more I thought about doing it myself. I measured, and mine is long enough to meet the minimum requirements.

"Yup," Baba says. Earlier he told me he thought it was a great idea. Mama was hesitant at first but then said she was fine with it, as long as I had thought it through. She also said to make sure it was something Bisma was comfortable with and that my cutting off my hair wouldn't make her unhappy in any way. I didn't tell my sisters or anyone else because I was afraid they might try to talk me out of it.

"You don't need to do this." Bisma puts her hand on mine.

"I know I don't. I want to. But I won't do it unless you say it's okay."

"Why is it up to me?" Bisma asks.

"Because I'm not trying to make you feel like I know what it's like to not have a choice to lose your hair. Or pretending to know what it's like to be in your shoes and to go through everything you're going through. You're the bravest person I've ever met, and I—" I get choked up and can't continue.

Bisma squeezes my hand tight and then runs her hand lightly over my hair.

"Thank you," she says. "I think it's nice you want to help somebody else going through this. I don't know if I'll wear a wig. But if I do, I want one with pretty hair like yours."

"So you want to do this?" Renee holds up the cape. "Ready?"

I take a deep breath.

"Ready."

43

It's honestly better in real life than the selfie you sent." Kayla checks my head out from all angles as we wait for the morning bell to ring. "Do you like it?"

"Not really," I admit. "It's going to take a while for me to get used to it. I cried last night when I was in bed and Bisma was asleep. I've had long hair forever and keep reaching up and then realizing there's nothing there."

"I think it's awesome," Lily says. "You look cool. And it's extra cool that it's not a regular haircut. You're doing something to make a difference."

"I hope so." Renee tried to give me a bit of a style, so it wasn't a straight buzz cut. I've got a longer piece that hangs in front over my eyes.

"What did your family think?"

"My parents were super positive about it. Bisma said she loved it and promised she wasn't just saying it. Maryam was in total shock and kept saying that she wished she had the guts to do it too. I think Aleeza had the best reaction, though."

"What did she say?"

"When she saw me, she yelled, 'Oh no! What did you do? Your hair's the prettiest thing about you!'"

We laugh over that. My friends know Aleeza and her brutal honesty well.

"You know that's not true, though, right?" Lily asks. "Your hair's pretty, but it's not the best thing about you."

"Thanks. When I grow it back, I'll appreciate it more and take better care of it," I say. "But until then, this is super easy to wash."

"Has anyone else seen it?" Lily asks. She doesn't say who she's thinking about, but I'm smart enough to know without asking. And I've been wondering myself what he'll think when he sees me.

"Only you guys. And my bus driver, who said she loved it." The words are barely out of my mouth when Kenzie and her crew pass by.

"Cute hair," Kenzie says in a way that sounds sincere. I thank her, wondering if she read my article, since she never acknowledged it. I didn't call her out specifically, or mention what she said to me, but it wouldn't take a rocket scientist to figure it out.

When I walk into the newspaper room during lunch, Ms. Levy does a major double take.

"Jameela! Wow! That's a new look for you," she says.

"I donated my hair to Wigs for Kids."

"Oh that doesn't surprise me. I should have known it had to be for something like that. Good for you! You're adorable." Ms. Levy beams at me. "Can you come into my office for a minute?"

I follow her into the office and settle into the chair I've come to know so well.

"You know, I've been reading your CaringBridge blog, and it's so moving. You really bring your sister's journey to life."

"Thanks."

"Your writing shines when it's about something you're passionate about. And I think the fund-raiser you mentioned in your last post, for the walk, is wonderful. I checked with the administration and got permission to spread the word to the school community through the PTA."

"That would be awesome! Bisma will be psyched. She's totally gotten into it. I'll share the link to our page with you."

"You know"—Ms. Levy grabs the last issue of the newspaper off her desk—"I have to admit: I finally understand why you've been unsatisfied with the paper." She pauses and then adds, "And I'm sorry that I haven't been more supportive of you."

"You didn't do anything," I say, and I mean it.

"No, I should have listened to you more about wanting to write about things that mattered to you. If they matter to you, you clearly have a gift for making them matter to others. That's the mark of a good journalist."

It feels strange to hear a teacher say she's wrong about something. That doesn't happen very often. But Ms. Levy is special. And not because her nails have tiny stars emblazoned on them.

"I was thinking that it would be lovely if you wrote a feature on your sister and this challenge for your family for the next issue. It would do a lot to help people understand what it's like to live with cancer, and to remember that it affects kids, too. You can add a bit about the walk, and mention how people can support it."

I don't tell Ms. Levy that I've already been thinking of a similar article on my own and hoping that Travis would get out of my way and let me write it. Instead, I let her think it's her idea.

"I could interview my sister and talk about the

things that she appreciates that other people do for her, and things she doesn't like. That way, if someone is in a similar situation where someone they love has cancer, they can have a better idea of what truly helps."

"That sounds perfect, Jameela." Ms. Levy grabs a tissue off her desk and dabs at her eyes. "You're learning a tremendous amount this year. And it's going to set you up nicely to be an effective editor next year."

Editor. I know I heard her correctly. But does she mean a regular section editor, or editor in chief? I don't want to push my luck, but I have to know.

"Ms. Levy, do you think I could maybe still be considered for editor in chief next year? Even though I messed up my last story?"

"Absolutely, hon. I think your idea to print an apology and make a commitment to honest reporting is the right call. And having a follow-up survey so students can share their own experiences with microaggressions is a good way to keep the issue in people's minds, and allow them to continue to think about it and learn."

Yes! I suppress a yell but grin so hard my face starts to hurt.

"I've got faith in you, Jameela. You'll go far in the field of journalism if you stick with it."

"The survey would be a lot easier if our paper went

digital," I blurt out. As much as I've wanted the paper to stay the way it's been—printed on paper—I think Ali might be right. "Right now you have to remember to save the paper, and then type the link into a computer. I don't know how many people will bother to do that."

"That's true," Ms. Levy muses. "But I thought you were with me on newspapers staying paper?"

"I love paper newspapers. I love the way they smell and the crinkly sound they make. But I think more kids will read ours if it's digital. We can add videos and other things that will make it more popular."

"Those are good points," Ms. Levy concedes. "Plus it'll cost less, so we won't need as many advertisers. Let's talk to the group next time we meet and think it through."

Ms. Levy is the best. Not only does she listen to what I have to say and take me seriously, she acts like my opinion counts for something. And she's going to help me get the word out about fund-raising for the walk, too.

I don't know how to thank Ms. Levy enough, so as we get up to leave, I give her a hug. She seems surprised at first, but then hugs me back, tight.

44

I spot Ali's backpack when I leave school. He's in line, waiting for his bus, so I tap him on the shoulder. He turns around halfway.

"Yeah?" he asks without really looking at me.

"Salaams."

"Blimey! It's you! What happened?" Now he's staring at me with a shocked expression.

Blood rushes to my face.

"I cut my hair."

"I can see that. But why?"

I start to sweat from embarrassment and want to kick myself for not walking by. The bus pulls up, and I try to sound casual as kids start to file on board.

"I donated it to a place that makes wigs for kids. See you later." I start to walk away.

Ali trails behind me instead of staying in his line.

"Don't you have to get the bus?" I ask as the other kids start to climb on.

"Forget the bus. What did you do? I can't believe you did that."

"Well, I did," I snap.

Ali smiles. "I'm not saying it's terrible."

Wait. What? Is that a compliment?

"You look like a proper rock star," Ali explains.

"Oh." I figure that's not a bad thing.

"Yeah," he says.

"Yeah," I repeat.

"How do you like it?" Ali asks.

"I don't know. I catch a reflection of myself and am like, 'Who is that?'"

"Trust me. You don't have anything to worry about. Long hair, short hair. Either way"—he winks—"you're ace."

"Very funny. I think you've got me confused for Maryam," I scoff. Ali may love to tease, but I'm not ready to make jokes about this yet.

Ali fumbles with the straps on his backpack for a bit

as he studies me with a puzzled expression. "You don't see it, do you?"

"What?"

"Maryam's a lovely girl. All of you Mirza sisters are. But I think you're the loveliest."

"Me?" This is the last thing I expected him to say. And I find it hard to believe.

"Yes, you, you muppet."

"But I always see you, um—"

"What?"

"You know, checking out Maryam."

"Do you?" Ali's cheeks turn red. "Well, she does do a lot to get checked out, doesn't she? With that stuff she puts on her face and the different hairstyles. She doesn't need it."

"I guess."

"Funny you noticed that, but not me noticing you."

I kick a crack in the sidewalk with my sneaker. This is not the reaction I imagined, and I have no idea what to say next, as my stomach flutters in an unexpected way.

"How's Bisma?" Ali changes the subject and breaks the awkward silence.

"She's feeling pretty good. She shaved her head completely. And she was going to try to go to school today for a couple hours."

"I'll come visit her soon. Or maybe now? I guess we both need a way to get home, right?" The buses have pulled out of the driveway, leaving us standing around with kids who are waiting in the carpool lane to get picked up.

"My mom can probably get us."

"I should jog home to get in shape. I'm trying out for Georgia Rush," Ali says. "Your little lecture did me some good."

"What?"

"The football club. Eli is on it. They're letting me try out next week. So thanks for straightening it out for me."

"Oh, awesome! That's really, really great." It makes me happy to hear that Ali's not quitting soccer. "And listen. I need your help with getting the word out about our fund-raiser on social media." I fill Ali in on my plans and invite him to walk with us for Light the Night.

"You know I'll be there. But wait, did you say . . . social media?" Ali feigns horror.

"Yes. It's not all bad," I concede. "Mama shared the link to the blog post about the walk on Facebook, and other people are sharing it. I think we'll have more people join us and donate if we get the word out that way."

"I'll share it too," Ali says. He stares at me again,

intently studying my face and hair in a way that makes me look down at my phone.

"Mama says she'll be here in fifteen minutes."

I wonder if Ali feels as uncomfortable as I do and if he's sweating too, until he speaks again.

"We're going to be okay, Jam. You, me, Bisma. All of us. We're going to be simply smashing. Like that hair-style."

Now I know he's teasing me for sure. So I punch him lightly in the shoulder as we lean together against the brick wall and wait for our ride.

45

I can't stop checking it every time I see an alert." Bisma clicks on her personal fund-raising page for the Light the Night walk.

"How much now?" Aleeza asks.

"Over a thousand dollars." I hear the amazement in Bisma's voice. "We already passed my goal."

"That's awesome!" Maryam cheers. "Who just gave?"

"I can't tell from the name." Bisma peers at the screen. "Maybe a friend of Mama's or Baba's from work?"

"Let me see." I get out of my chair and sit next to Bisma on the couch.

It's only been a week since we officially kicked off the fund-raising campaign, after first writing about the walk on CaringBridge. Bisma and I set up her welcome page on the Light the Night website, where we wrote an introduction, added photos, and set her fund-raising goal.

"I think Ali's video made the difference," Maryam says. "It's been viewed hundreds of times already. And look how many likes it got on Facebook."

I'm pretty sure Maryam is right. After we were done setting up the page, I texted the link to Ali. He showed up at our front door a few hours later, said we needed a video to go with the campaign, and filmed an interview with Bisma on his phone. Then he recorded a bunch of extra scenes of Bisma playing the piano, cuddling a stuffed toy, and coloring with Aleeza. Bisma said she felt like a movie star when he made her change into three different outfits so it would look like they were recording the video on different days.

The next morning he came up to me and casually handed me his phone before school started.

"Take a look," he said.

I was completely blown away. In just a few hours, he'd managed to put together a professional-looking video, complete with background music and Bisma's voice speaking over parts of the footage. At the end, Bisma looks directly into the camera and shyly asks for people to join her on the walk and support her campaign "to Light the Night and fight the darkness of cancer."

"This is incredible," I told Ali. "You're so good! You should direct movies in real life!"

"I hope it helps" was all he said, but his eyes were dancing. After I showed his work to Ms. Levy, she said she was going to ask him to join the video and production club at school. I'm going to push him to sign up.

"All of Mama and Baba's friends shared the link to the video and the page on Facebook and Instagram," Maryam continues. "Mama said Uncle Saeed's relatives in London contributed, and so did some old friends of theirs who live in California who they haven't seen in twenty years, and a bunch of their cousins in Pakistan who we hardly know."

"Everyone's being so nice," Bisma says. "You should see these comments."

She hands me the computer, and I start to read the notes that some of the people who donated have left. As I scroll, I notice messages from people of all ages and faiths, some I recognize and others I don't. All of them use positive phrases like "God is great," "Sending you healing wishes," and "Keep fighting!" I recognize the names of Kayla's and Lily's families, Ms. Levy, our neighbors, and even Miss Jasmin. I pause when I see the most recent name: the Hudson Family.

"Oh. Wow. I think this is the editor of my school paper."

"Travis?" Aleeza asks. "The guy you don't like?"

"Well, I didn't like him before," I admit. "But we're learning to get along."

Travis was completely on board when I told him about my idea to write a feature on Bisma for the next issue of the paper. Plus he agreed with me about needing to make the paper digital to attract more readers. Maybe it won't be so bad working together for the rest of the year. I scroll down to the messages and read, "Sending all our best wishes to you, Bisma." I'm touched by his family's kindness and generosity, and know it must have been his idea, since his parents have never met us.

After Bisma was home from the hospital, Baba and I sat down and finally talked about my article debacle and everything that had happened with Travis and Ali. I was a little offended at first when Baba started laughing about the version mix-up. But then he kept cracking jokes about it until I started giggling too.

"Mistakes happen, Jam," he said after teasing me about it for a while. "The important thing is that you learn from them."

"I know. But I wanted the article to be extra awesome for you. I didn't get you a gift when you left," I confessed.

"You don't need to get me anything," Baba said. "You are all the gift I ever need. Except now that I think of it, I wouldn't mind an extra-awesome welcome-home issue of the *Mirza Memos*, please. And some pancakes."

I promised it would be the best issue yet.

"Ali's mom gave a donation too," Bisma says. "And we get to meet her this weekend."

Ali has been practically giddy with excitement over his mom and sister arriving. I can't wait to meet them, and Mama's already planning a nice dinner for them on Sunday. But I remember that soon after Ali's family will be reunited, ours is going to be splintered again.

Baba has to go back to Abu Dhabi on Tuesday to finish up his work there and pack up his things, since he left to come here so suddenly. The good news is that he's starting a new contract here in December. Mama told me it's less money, but it's for two years and good enough for us to be fine financially.

"I'll put off replacing the family room furniture again," she said with a laugh. But my sisters and I were relieved. Worn out or not, it's the furniture we've grown up with and what feels like home. And that means I get to keep my chair.

My chest tightens as I imagine saying good-bye to Baba again. So I force myself to stop thinking about that and to try to enjoy this moment. I glance over at him, sitting at the dining table with Mama, drinking chai and relaxing. I notice that there are more grays in his hair, and I wonder if he'll name them Bisma.

Bisma hits my arm as she gets another message on her fund-raising page. Aleeza is reading a graphic novel in the corner. Maryam is sitting with her phone in her hand, but instead of looking at it, she's staring into the room with a thoughtful expression on her face. Our eyes meet, and I know she's thinking the same thing as me. We're here together—all of us—and that is everything.

46

It's a warm, humid night, despite it being the beginning of November. We've been anticipating this night for weeks, and it's finally here: the Light the Night walk.

There's a large stage set up on one end of Peachtree Street to kick off the event. Since Bisma raised over three thousand dollars in total from three continents, she is an official Champion for Cures. Plus, she was chosen by the coordinators to be onstage for the lighting ceremony. At first she refused, saying that she felt too nervous about being in front of everyone, but we finally convinced her to do it.

Bisma waits on one side of the stage while a news anchor from WSB-TV welcomes everyone to the walk.

Then a woman from the Leukemia & Lymphoma Society explains that the money everybody raised goes to fund lifesaving cancer research and supports families on their cancer journeys.

I feel a hand slip into mine as I watch. It's Maryam, who's standing next to me. Mama is behind us with Ali's mom, his sister Zoya, and Aleeza. Ali is standing on the other side of me.

The host tells the story of someone who was lost to cancer and introduces her sister, who is walking in her memory. The sister lights a gold lantern, and everyone in the crowd who is honoring a loved one lights matching gold lanterns. There's a heavy moment of silence while some people lock arms and hug each other.

Next the woman calls Bisma to step forward. As our sister courageously stands in front of hundreds; the lady tells Bisma's story of her fight against lymphoma. When she explains that Bisma has completed two rounds of chemotherapy and that her scans came back clear last week, everyone claps and cheers, and Bisma smiles brightly. The lady goes on to say that Bisma's fight isn't over and that she has two more rounds of chemo to go, but that we are all rooting for her. My eyes fill up, and I feel Maryam squeeze my hand. When we got the news of her scans, we all wept with gratitude. Mama immediately gave a donation to the poor, sadaqa, to thank God for his mercy.

Bisma lights the white lantern she is holding, and all the survivors in the audience do the same. I take photos of her on the stage, wearing her Light the Night T-shirt and cap and triumphantly waving her lantern high.

Finally, the host invites the third person on the stage to come up, and while he shifts his weight from one leg to the other, she talks about how he is walking in support of his son who is battling leukemia and thanks those of us who are here to support others. After he lights his red lantern, I light mine, along with everyone else on Team Bisma, and the crowd erupts into loud applause and whistles.

Bisma comes off the stage, and we smother her in a group hug, and then follow the crowd to start the walk. It's a beautiful sight as what appear to be a thousand lanterns—white, gold, and red—light the night sky up and down Peachtree Street.

"This is incredible," Maryam says in a low voice, as if she doesn't want to disrupt the magic we're witnessing. "You can feel the energy in the air."

"I know," I agree. "It's not just the lights. It's all the people."

I look around at everyone who is walking with us. Blended into a crowd of hundreds, at least thirty people from Team Bisma surround us, wearing their matching T-shirts and wristbands, and holding their red lanterns.

Aleeza and Zoya are walking close to Bisma, carrying the banner we made. The two of them decorated it over the past week, and it's been cute to watch them become instant friends. They're almost the same size, although Zoya is older, and I can see how Bisma might have reminded Ali of his sister, minus the British accent. Zoya shares Bisma's innocent look and shy smile. Ali's mother and Mama have quickly bonded too, and they are together now with Farah Auntie. Ali's mom, who I call Zarina Auntie, has an easy laugh and expressive face, and I can see where Ali gets his sense of humor.

Ms. Levy's here, walking in a pink baseball cap and holding hands with her husband. He's carrying a gold lantern, to honor his uncle who died of leukemia. I've thought a lot about what she said: how I can make a difference by writing about things that are important to the people I love and doing what I can to make them matter to other people. That's the type of journalist I want to be. And even if I don't win any awards, being here tonight and getting everyone to join us and contribute feels better than any prize or gold plaque ever could.

Lily and Kayla are giggling a few rows behind me

and have probably noted with glee that Ali hasn't left my side. As I look up at him, he smiles, his dark eyes filled with emotion.

"If I find something like this to honor my dad, will you walk with me?" he asks, making me choke up for the third time tonight.

"Of course," I promise. I'm missing Baba so much right now, since he's back in Abu Dhabi, but he's close to getting back home for good. It won't be soon enough.

Bisma turns her head, searching the crowd until her eyes meet mine. The light that was missing after she got sick is back, and she seems much more like herself again. Although she has a long road ahead, and we have to wait and pray that the cancer doesn't return, for now we're celebrating. Bisma seems stronger and more optimistic than ever. Her cheerful spirit makes it easier for all of us, even as cancer remains a big part of our lives.

"Thank you," she mouths to me with a face full of gratitude.

"We did it," I mouth back.

I've been thinking for a while now about the article I'm going to write for the next issue of the *Crossing*. Filled with emotion, I draft the starting lines in my mind:

I never thought something terrible could make me better

in any way. But sometimes it takes something bad to happen to make you appreciate the good things you have in your life. I've learned a lot of things since my sister was diagnosed with cancer. For starters, I know how terrifying it is to imagine the worst things happening to someone you love so much, and how helpless you can feel while you watch. But I also saw how strong my sister has been through this test, and realize you should never underestimate anyone. I had to learn not to smother her, and to try to turn my anger and fear into something positive. No one can fight cancer alone, so I'm going to hold on to my sister as hard as I can and help her keep fighting with everything I've got. . . .

ACKNOWLEDGMENTS

My sister owned a worn copy of *Little Women* that I read over and over again when I was growing up. Eventually, when I knew most of the story by heart, I'd flip it open to a random page and start reading from there. My family could trace where I had been in our home last based on where the book was sitting.

Something about the story deeply resonated with me, as a daughter, sister, friend, and someone trying to navigate two cultures and a society I didn't feel I neatly fit into. I found parallels between my life and the four sisters on the pages who were living in a different era, and lost myself in their hopes and dreams.

That's why I was overjoyed when I spoke to my amazing editor, Zareen Jaffery, about an idea to write a story inspired by my favorite book of all time, and she shared my enthusiasm for the project. It was a dream come true, and I felt enormously grateful to her. But then, when it was time to write it, my nerves kicked in. How would I even begin to pay tribute to a classic that is beloved by so many?

Thankfully I had plenty of support along the way. My sister talked through my outline with me when I was ready to give up and helped me reimagine it as a middle-grade novel. My wonderful writing group, the talented Ann McCallum, Laura Gehl, and Joan Waites, gave me their constructive feedback, sometimes with ridiculously short turnaround times. The incredible author N. H. Senzai generously shared her insights, challenging me to do more. My friend Afgen Sheikh listened to my ideas, read my final draft, and assured me I didn't need to start over.

I'm indebted to Sayyid Tahir Ali for working with me from London to make sure Ali sounded authentically British. Thank you for your patience and good humor, especially when I got my notions of Briticisms from old-school cartoons. (Guess what, Bugs Bunny fans? British people don't actually call sugar cubes "lumps"!) I also was lucky to receive the valuable input of two bright young people who inspired characters in the book, Lily Scheckner and Kayla Pak, and the advice of my thoughtful nephew, Yusuf Khan.

My agent, Matthew Elblonk, believed in this story from the outset and has cheered me on ever since. Thank you for all that you do for me, and for the free therapy sessions.

Like always, my family was there for me. My mother helped keep me on track, brainstormed titles, and gave me advice like no one else can. I'm grateful to my siblings and siblings-in-law for rooting for me. My husband, Farrukh, read every word of my drafts and shared his ideas. I owe so much to him and think he might have secretly majored in English. And my sons, Bilal and Humza, provided feedback and hugs when I needed them and tried to make it easier for me to juggle being a writer and a mother. I'm more thankful for and proud of you two than anything in the world.

This book would not have been possible without the Kilner family. When I decided to write about Hodgkin's lymphoma, I reached out to my neighbor and friend Maura Kilner, whose daughter Meaghan was undergoing treatment at the time. Both Maura and Meaghan's openness and generosity in sharing their experiences were more than I could have ever asked for. Meaghan not only thoughtfully answered my many questions about her journey as a cancer survivor, but as an avid reader she also read my draft and offered valuable editorial notes.

Meaghan Kilner, you are one of the strongest people I have ever had the pleasure of knowing, a model of grace and courage, and a true inspiration. I pray for your continued health and strength. And I ask everyone to please consider supporting Meaghan's organization of choice, the Leukemia and Lymphoma Society, to help fund cancer research and support others in their fight against blood cancers. You can learn more at www.lls.org.

I still have my sister's copy of *Little Women*. She eventually gave it to me, knowing how much it meant to me. Thank you, Andala, for always looking out for your little sis. You inspired the love Jameela has for Bisma.

Finally, I must thank you, dear reader. I'm honored you chose my book and hope you will connect to Jameela and her sisters, and that they make a place in your heart. There is more to each of our stories than we realize sometimes, and we need them to offer each other comfort, hope, and companionship. I hope you will find the courage to tell yours.